When a stranger knocks on his door and promises to lead
him to hidden treasure, twelve-year-old Rudi is skeptical.
And he's even more suspicious when the stranger proclaims
that the jewels belonged to the legendary Hansel. Sure,
Rudi's heard stories: the witch, the oven, the sister named
Gretel. But he never fully believed they were real.
Until now . . .

Don't miss these other Further Tales:

The Thief and the Beanstalk

The Brave Apprentice

Coming Soon:

The Mirror's Tale

The Eye of the Warlock

P. W. CATANESE

ALADDIN PAPERBACKS
NEW YORK   LONDON   TORONTO   SYDNEY

The Eye of the Warlock

This book is a work of fiction. Any references to historical events, real people, or real locales are used fictitiously. Other names, characters, places, and incidents are the product of the author's imagination, and any resemblance to actual events or locales or persons, living or dead, is entirely coincidental.

🐫 ALADDIN PAPERBACKS
An imprint of Simon & Schuster Children's Publishing Division
1230 Avenue of the Americas, New York, NY 10020
Text copyright © 2005 by P. W. Catanese
All rights reserved, including the right of reproduction
in whole or in part in any form.
ALADDIN PAPERBACKS and colophon are registered
trademarks of Simon & Schuster, Inc.
Designed by Tom Daly
The text of this book was set in Adobe Jenson.
Manufactured in the United States of America
First Aladdin Paperbacks edition November 2005
2 4 6 8 10 9 7 5 3 1
Library of Congress Control Number 2005923514
ISBN-13: 978-0-689-87175-7
ISBN-10: 0-689-87175-9

For my parents
Ralph and Muriel

CHAPTER 1

Rudi had a feeling that something was wrong as soon as he returned from the village.

The little girls were nowhere in sight. "Elsebeth? Lucie?" he called. But neither of them answered. A warm, prickly feeling swept across the back of his neck.

He went to the tiny house on the edge of the forest. This rickety place had stood here for many years, passed from one woodsman to the next kinsman who was witless or desperate enough to take on this trade. Witless, in Uncle Hempel's case.

Hempel's ax was gone from its usual place on the wall, so Rudi was sure he'd gone into the woods. *He probably took the girls with him because I wasn't here to help,* he thought.

"Aunt Agnes?" he called, to no reply. It was just as well. He never welcomed a conversation with her. *I guess Aunt Agnes went along to gather wood. But why? She never does that. . . .*

He ran to the mouth of the forest path that was blazed and cleared by generations of woodsmen. It was wide at first, then narrowed as shrubs and trees encroached from either side, until the shadowy corridor withered to nothing, miles deep in the murky interior of the woods.

Cupping his hands, Rudi shouted, "Uncle Hempel! Elsie and Lucie! Are you there? Do you need some help?"

Nobody answered. Rudi frowned and ran his fingers through his white-blond hair. He suddenly realized what was troubling him: a notion that had been swimming just under the surface of his mind now leaped up and revealed itself like a fish. It was the legend of something that supposedly happened many years before, to a brother and sister who lived in this very house. *Don't be silly*, he thought, forcing his thoughts away from that tale.

Sounds came from the forest: twigs snapping, leaves rustling, and the voice of his aunt, harsh as always. He took a deep breath and let it out slowly.

Aunt Agnes came out first, carrying only a bundle of sticks. There was a look on her face that Rudi didn't like at all—a secret, satisfied smile. Uncle Hempel came out next. His wide-bladed ax was slung from his leather belt. He bore a large stack of logs on his shoulder and a cow's vacant stare on his face.

Rudi looked behind them. First he expected to see the girls come out of the path. Then he hoped. Then he prayed.

"Where are the girls?" Rudi said to his aunt in a voice

that cracked. He ran to catch up with her. "Where are Lucie and Elsie?"

Agnes looked back at the trees, and her eyebrows rose theatrically. "What? They're not here? They headed back before we did."

Rudi clenched his hands so tightly that the nails bit into the flesh of his palms. "Alone? You let them come back *alone?*"

Agnes stepped closer. Rudi was a boy of average size, so she loomed over him, a full head taller. "Don't take that tone with me, Rudiger. And calm yourself. The girls just went off to pick flowers or have one of their foolish games. That's all they ever want to do, anyway. Never work, only play."

"They *didn't* come out. I would have *seen* them," Rudi said. A hot fury erupted inside him, and his fists began to shake.

Agnes let her bundle of sticks drop to the ground at his feet. "Did you sell that oak at Waldrand? I hope you got a fair price, not like last time. But that's what happens when you trust a boy with a man's job." She wiped her hands on the front of her dress.

Suddenly the unexpected errand she'd sent him on made sense to Rudi. "You *wanted* me gone all day, didn't you? So I wouldn't be there to help the girls!" He turned to his uncle, who'd caught up to them now and dropped his bundle next to Agnes's. "Where are they, Uncle? What happened to Lucie and Elsie?"

"Oh. Well, Rudi, Agnes thought . . . ," Hempel stammered, but Agnes interrupted him with a shriek.

"Hush, you fool! I already told him, the girls came back before us. They're around somewhere. Now leave us be and stack this wood, boy."

"No!" Rudi cried, kicking at the bundle. He knew he was shouting like a madman now, but he couldn't help it. Agnes might swat him with a switch, or refuse to give him his dinner, but he didn't care anymore. "I've heard you talk about them. I heard you tell Uncle there are too many mouths to feed. Now you've lost them in the woods. I know you did! It was *your* idea!" He jabbed a finger at Agnes, then whirled to face Hempel. "But why'd you let her do it? What's happened to you, Uncle Hempel?" Hempel chewed on a knuckle and stared at the ground.

Rudi ran to the cottage and threw the door open so hard that it nearly cracked as it struck the wall. His breath hissed in and out through his teeth as he grabbed his pack and stuffed a pair of blankets into it, along with his tinderbox, a knife, and his small ax. He dashed to the kitchen and added some fruits, a wedge of cheese, and the last of the bread.

When he turned around, he saw Agnes in the doorway. "What do you think you're doing? Put that food back; it's all we've got!" She spread her arms to block the way out.

"I'm going to find them."

"They're not lost!"

"They are so!" Rudi swung the pack over his shoulder. "I wish you'd never met my uncle." He jumped onto a chair and from there sprang through the open kitchen window.

Outside, Hempel sat on a stump, moaning and rubbing at the dampness on his cheeks. When he saw Rudi run by, his broad shoulders began to quake.

How much sunlight left? Rudi wondered. *An hour or two maybe.* He ran down the path, wondering where the girls might be. After a while he stopped and shouted their names, but the only answer came from the birds that were startled into flight, and the tiny unseen creatures that scurried in the brush.

Farther in, Rudi decided. Agnes wasn't kind, but she was clever. She would have lured the girls deep into the forest, where they'd have no chance of finding their way home. *Just like what happened to—what were their names? Hansel. That was the boy, and his sister was Gretel. They were relatives of his who lived in the same house many years ago. One day they'd been taken into the woods and told to wait by the fire for their mother and father to get them when the work was done. But their parents never came. And then it got dark. Like it is right now.*

He shouted again, and put his hands behind his ears to listen. For a moment, he thought he heard something. But no, it was only an owl's cry.

Rudi ran farther and came to a stream with footprints in the muddy bank. There were two small pairs of prints among them, but they only pointed in one direction: deeper into the woods. He leaped across and ran on, looking left and right for the place where Agnes might have led the girls off the trail.

He stopped at last and leaned against a tree, hugging his stomach and drawing air into his aching lungs. His legs and arms might be strong from his days of cutting and hauling wood, but he'd never run this far in his life. When his breathing slowed, he shouted once more: "Lucie! Elsebeth!"

He heard nothing. But he smelled something. He tilted his head back and inhaled deeply, turned to where the scent was strongest, and sniffed again.

A fire. Somewhere ahead. Rudi stepped off the trail, keenly aware that it would be easy to get lost. He'd be walking away from the setting sun, so he could find the path again by heading back toward it, obviously. Or later, by keeping the North Star to his right. He smacked his fist against his thigh. Why hadn't he taught the girls how to find their way through the woods? There were so many things he knew and never shared.

The smoky scent grew stronger as he trotted east, his shadow stretching long and thin before him. He called again and again, but still no one answered. *Maybe they're asleep by the fire,* he thought, trying to reassure himself. He saw smoke through the trees and sprinted the rest of the way, until he stood in a clearing with the smoldering remains of a fire in front of him. But the girls were not there.

Rudi noticed something on the ground near the embers. It was a wreath made from wild vines twisted together. Lucie and Elsebeth surely made it; it was the sort of thing they would do to pass the time. Rudi picked it up and clutched it against his chest. He shouted their names again and again in every direction, until his throat was raw and his voice grew weak.

"Oh, no," he moaned. He kicked at the embers, and sparks flew toward the dimming sky. They were out there somewhere, sweet Lucie and serious Elsie, only six and seven years old. But which way? He was no hunter who could track their steps through the woods, reading the trodden grass or broken stems or other subtle clues. Besides, it would be too dark to see anything at all before long. He thought of them lost among the trees, holding on to one another in the black of night, and fought to push that image from his mind.

There was one thing he could do: Build up the fire again, until it roared so high it could be seen for miles in the night. *Yes, they'll see it and come back*, he thought. He gathered twigs and sticks and piled them on the embers—it would be easier than starting a new fire with his flint and steel.

The bits of wood smoldered and burst into flame under his coaxing breath, and soon a modest fire blazed again. He needed more fuel now, the biggest, driest branches he could find. At the edge of the clearing Rudi saw a dead branch jutting from the trunk of a tree. He seized it and wrenched it off, grunting through his clenched teeth. The branch was long, and he stomped on it to break it into smaller pieces. Somehow it felt good to break it, and Rudi wanted to go on stomping until only sawdust was left, and keep on stomping until the whole forest lay in splinters.

"How could they do this?" he screamed. It occurred to him that people could be far crueler than he'd ever believed possible. A raw and powerful kind of anger that he'd never known before roared inside him. He was hardly aware that he'd picked up a broken length of the dead limb and was smashing it against the tree, sending chips and bits of bark flying.

And then he heard a voice, thin and reedy and high, from the shadows.

"Are you looking for the girls?"

Rudi froze. He could suddenly hear the thump of his heart inside his ears. It was almost night now, and more light came from the fire than the sky. Between the trees, he spied a pale spectral face with dark eyes staring back.

The voice came again. "I said, are you looking for the girls?"

Rudi had to swallow before he could answer. "Who is that? Who are you?"

The face vanished behind a thick tree, and came out

on the other side, a little closer. It seemed to float among the shadows. "You are Rudi, aren't you? They said you would come."

"Where are the girls? If you have them, let them go." Rudi opened the top of his bag and pulled out the little ax.

"Put that away. Don't be afraid. The girls are safe, but they're not here."

"I'm not afraid!" Rudi shouted, but his brittle voice betrayed him. "But who are you? Why won't you let me see you?" He squeezed the handle of the ax, but that didn't stop it from shaking.

The pale face hung in the shadows for a moment, and then equally white hands reached up and drew a hood over its head. The stranger stepped into the orange light of the fire. It was a woman, Rudi realized; he could tell from her slender hands and the way she moved. He should have known already from her voice—it was hoarse, but still a woman's. Her head was bowed so the drooping hood concealed her features. She wore a long cloak made of deerskin dyed dark brown, almost black. In one hand she held a bow, and he saw the feathered ends of a bouquet of arrows over her shoulder. Rudi lowered the ax to his side.

"My name is Marusch. Now come, we should leave this place," she said.

"Why? I'm not going anywhere until you show your face!"

"Ill-mannered boy. You may regret what you've asked,"

she said. The pale, long-fingered hands rose again and pushed the hood back.

Rudi gasped. He couldn't help it. Only the brown hair that hung past her shoulders in braids seemed normal. Everything else was wrong. Her skin was pure white, as if the sun never touched it. Coarse but sparse hair sprouted all over her face, even her forehead. And her mouth was the worst of all. The lips were shriveled and drawn back to bare a mouthful of long, red-stained teeth.

"Go away—leave me alone!" Rudi whined. He stepped backward and raised his ax to ward off the ghastly stranger.

"I warned you," she said. "But now you must . . ." Her voice trailed off and she looked past Rudi. A sound was approaching: footsteps in the woods.

"Elsie? Lucie?" Rudi called out weakly. It was more a question than a hail.

"It isn't them," Marusch whispered. "It was a mistake to build the fire again—now follow me!" Without waiting for a reply, she turned and hastened into the trees. Rudi paused for a moment and listened with failing courage to the approaching footsteps. They were too heavy and too many to belong to the girls. And something was wrong with the sound, somehow. It was unlike the steps of men. Now that he listened more carefully, Rudi heard other, unsettling noises mingled with the steps: hissing and gurgling.

Before whatever it was entered the clearing and saw him, he snatched up his pack and ran after Marusch. In the dim light, he could just make out her form. "Please, Marusch—slow down!" he called as loudly as he dared. She stopped and waited, then gestured for him to join her behind a fallen tree. Crouching low, she tapped a finger against her drawn-back lips. They hid quietly, and she peered over the top of the log every now and then.

"It is safe," she said finally.

"Who were they?"

"Strange beings that have begun to prowl these woods," she replied. "Now come." And she was on the move again, darting through the trees.

Isn't that a thing. That's what Uncle Hempel always said when something out of the ordinary happened. He'd be saying it now for sure, if he was trying to follow this mysterious woman through the dark forest. Rudi wondered how she could know where she was going when he could barely see her from just a few steps behind. Marusch didn't move in a straight line. Instead she weaved left and right, so that he was soon irretrievably lost, with no hope of finding the path again. He began to wonder if he was being led into a trap, a trap that had already taken Lucie and Elsebeth.

Rudi nearly slammed into Marusch as she stopped at last in front of a great evergreen tree with a silvery gray trunk so wide a dozen men could have been concealed behind it. "Here," she said.

"What? Where?"

She pointed up, and Rudi saw a narrow ladder made of cord and wooden rungs that disappeared into the darkness above. "Go on, I will follow," Marusch said.

"Me? Uh, why don't you go first?"

She stared at him, and Rudi had to turn away from her pale, red-toothed face.

"So you fear to turn your back to me," Marusch said. "But weren't you behind me all this way? I only meant to stay below you, so I could help you find your footing. But as you wish, Rudi—I will go first."

She went up nimbly and swiftly, as if eager to put some distance between them, and soon disappeared into the branches above. Rudi sighed deeply. He climbed after her, moving deliberately. The ladder that had seemed so steady under her hands and feet wobbled and swayed with his every move. He climbed through the bristling boughs until he was high above the ground and the trunk had tapered to half its size at the base. Overhead a wide flat shape came into view, so well concealed by the needled branches that he never could have seen it from the ground below. It was a platform that completely encircled the tree. Near the trunk there was a square black hole through which the ladder disappeared. Rudi climbed through the opening, and was surprised to find a roof over his head and walls around him. Marusch was waiting, and once he arrived she drew the ladder up, turning it like a scroll in her hands.

The room was dimly lit by a simple oil lamp that hung from a chain. It was just bright enough for Rudi to see Lucie and Elsebeth lying motionless on a mat in the corner. "*What have you done to them?*" he shouted, whirling to face Marusch.

"Quiet—you'll wake them."

But Lucie was already rising and rubbing her eyes with her tiny fists. She saw them and was suddenly awake. "Rudi! Oh Marusch, you found him!" And then she and Elsebeth sprang to their feet.

Rudi caught the leaping girls in his arms and staggered, laughing, under their weight. "That's right, she found me," he said. He looked at Marusch. It was hard to read the emotions on her disfigured face, because her shriveled lips couldn't close over her crimson teeth. Her mouth appeared to smile. But there was sadness in her eyes.

"I'm sorry I was suspicious," he said to her, bending his knees to lower the girls to the floor. "You scared me. . . ."

Marusch turned her face away. "I scare most people."

Rudi winced. "Not like that. You just came out of nowhere. And I was worried about the girls."

"You don't scare me, Marusch," Elsebeth said.

"Or me," said Lucie. Rudi had his hands on the girls' shoulders, and he gave them a gentle squeeze.

"But Rudi," Lucie said, frowning, "did you find Aunt

Agnes and Uncle Hempel? They must have gotten lost. We waited by the fire, but they didn't come back. We tried to find them, but we couldn't, and then Marusch heard us calling."

"Don't worry about your aunt and uncle," Rudi replied, more coldly than he intended. He didn't see any reason to tell the girls the ugly truth just yet. Lucie had no idea she and her sister had been abandoned, he could see that. But Elsebeth peered at him with her lips pressed together and trembling. Wise Elsie; she suspected. "Yes, they got lost," Rudi told Lucie. "But they found their way back, and sent me to find you." Lucie leaned against him and hugged him anew, while Elsebeth brought the back of one thumb to her mouth and bit it softly.

"Marusch, can you help us find the way home?" Rudi asked.

"I know your village. Yes, I will bring you back to your path. But not until dawn. It isn't safe for you to travel by night."

Rudi remembered those footsteps in the gloom, and the strange gurgling noises that came with them. He decided she was probably right.

When the girls dozed again, Rudi stood and stretched and took a closer look around the little house. The trunk of the evergreen passed through the floor and out the thatched ceiling. When he walked around the tree, he saw a hammock slung in the corner. Near it was a wooden chest and a small table, holding only a hairbrush made of ivory with most of its teeth broken away. He also noticed a jug of water, and a basin.

Clothes hung from pegs on the wall. Some were made from the skins of animals. Others were the kind that regular village folk wore, but most of these were too tattered and threadbare to be useful. Rudi's mouth dropped at the corners. The clothes seemed to whisper a story, about a woman who lived among other people long ago, until she was banished—or fled—to a lonely existence in the woods. *Because of the way she looked.*

A breeze whistled through the windows, strong with the scent of pine. The tree swayed in the wind, and the house rocked with it, creaking all the while. Rudi had never been on the deck of a ship in the ocean before, but he imagined it felt and sounded just like this.

Besides the hole in the floor, now covered by a trapdoor, there was only one way out of the house: through another doorway that was covered by a draped rectangle of deer hide. Marusch had left through that door. Rudi pushed the skin aside and walked out onto a covered porch that faced a dense curtain of green.

Marusch was there, leaning against the rail, working by the light of a single candle. At her feet were bundles of sticks bound firmly together. Ash saplings, Rudi noted with a woodsman's practiced eye. They were a yard long and as slender as his little finger. They looked like they'd been selected for their straightness. She held one sapling and peeled away the few bits of bark that were still on it, exposing the pale wood underneath. She raised it to her eyes, looked down the length of it, and flexed it to straighten it further.

"Making arrows, right?" Rudi asked. She glanced at him, nodded, and picked another sapling from the pile.

"I know lots about wood. If you run out of ash, try birch. The forest is full of birch, and that makes good arrows too," Rudi said. She nodded again, without looking away from her work.

Rudi drummed on his thigh with his fingers and blew a puff of air out of the corner of his mouth. He looked around the porch. There was a simple kitchen here, with a small iron stove and shelves lined with jars and boxes and bowls. At the other end was a bench with tools for woodworking and stitching garments.

He looked up and saw another ladder leading higher into the great tree where Marusch had built her home, a majestic pine that towered above its neighbors.

"So . . . this is where you live?" he asked, and this time she simply turned and regarded him with her head tilted and her eyebrows raised.

"Right," he said. "Dumb question. Of course you live here. It was smart to build in an evergreen—the house will always be hidden, even in winter."

"You should rest," Marusch told him. She picked up her bow and slung a quiver full of arrows over her shoulder.

"But—where are you going?"

"Hunting," she said.

"Now?"

"Yes. The night is my time. If you are hungry, you will find berries and nuts and mushrooms in those jars. So eat if you must. Then rest, because we will leave before the sun rises high." Without another word, she slipped into the first room and disappeared down the ladder.

CHAPTER 2

They followed Marusch through the forest, the girls walking between her and Rudi. She led them straight for a while, until her tree was out of sight. Then she took an abrupt turn to the left, and the right, and the left once more. From the faint glow of the sun that hadn't yet risen, Rudi could judge which way they were heading: south, west, south, east, north, west, south, west . . . It seemed like Marusch was guiding them through a labyrinth that only she could see.

They walked by a leaning tree that had toppled some time ago, only to be caught in the considerate branches of its neighboring oak. Rudi frowned at it. They'd passed it already on this journey.

Just when he was about to call to Marusch to ask if the girls could rest, she stopped. Rudi stepped behind her and whispered over her shoulder, so the girls would not hear. "Marusch, you don't have to confuse us like this. We won't come and look for you if you don't want us to. I promise."

She turned to face him. The sun had not risen yet, but this was the strongest light he'd seen her in so far. Determined not to look away, Rudi kept his gaze fixed on her dark blue eyes.

"Never come back," she said. "Or tell anyone about me."

"Oh, but Marusch," cried Elsebeth, "we want to see you again!"

Lucie tugged on her cloak. "Yes, you must be lonely. Rudi, did she tell you we're the first people to visit her in years?"

"No, she didn't," Rudi said. "Marusch, let us thank you by helping you. There must be things you need that we could bring you."

"I need nothing," she said. The sun was rising now, and its first rays pierced the narrow spaces between the trunks of the trees. Marusch turned her back and lifted her hood to shield her eyes.

"Is something wrong?" Rudi asked.

"I can't bear the sun," she replied. "It stings my eyes and burns my skin. It is time I left you."

"Leave us? But how will we find our way home?"

"If only your eyes were as mighty as your mouth, boy. Look around you." She used her bow to gesture to her right. Rudi saw a path—*their* path—just a few strides away.

From a pouch at her side Marusch pulled out a long and narrow piece of blue stained glass, like the kind Rudi had once seen in a church window in a faraway village. It had strips of cloth tied to holes at both ends. Marusch brought the glass to her eyes and secured it by knotting the strips behind her head. When she turned to face them again, the girls giggled at the sight of her.

Now that Rudi couldn't see her eyes, he couldn't imagine how Marusch was reacting to the girls' laughter. She simply said, "Good-bye," and turned to leave. But before she could take a second step, Lucie and Elsebeth ran to her and hugged her tight around the waist. She patted them on their heads, gently pried them away, and walked into the trees.

"There must be something we can give you," Rudi called after her.

"Solitude," she called over her shoulder. Then she was gone.

"We'll never see her again," Lucie mourned in her tiny, soft voice.

"It isn't fair," Elsebeth said, staring after her.

Rudi noticed an unusual rock next to the path, at the very spot where Marusch had left them. It was as tall as he and nearly round, with a wide vein of quartz running across it. It was cracked in half, with an inch-wide gap down the middle.

"Girls," he said, "don't forget this stone."

They stood at the edge of the woods, still in the shadows, and stared out into the brilliant sunlit meadow. Hempel was outside the house, swinging his ax with his brawny arms. The sound came toward them every time he propped another short length of wood on the scarred tree stump, and split it under his blade: *Thwock!*

Lucie tugged at Rudi's sleeve. "Why are we waiting?"

Rudi took a deep breath and let it escape through his nose. *We're waiting because I don't know what to do or what to say*, he thought. He'd been thinking about that since Marusch left them on the path, and he still hadn't the slightest idea. Should they say nothing and pretend it never happened? Would Agnes even let them come back? And where would they go if she didn't? There was nobody he could think of who would take them in. No one in the village wanted three more mouths to feed.

Thwock!

He bent his knees to look the girls in the eye. "Ready?"

"I don't want to go back," Elsebeth said through clenched teeth. Lucie's mouth trembled, and she blinked furiously as her eyes began to water.

They knew. Both of them knew.

Thwock!

Rudi took their hands, squeezing gently. He didn't want to talk about what Agnes had done, but he had to say something. "It'll be all right, girls. I'll take care of you. And I'll try to find someplace for us to go. A place where we can be happy and safe. Until then, stay close to me. Understand? Don't go anywhere without me. And don't trust Aunt Agnes or Uncle Hempel. Or any other grown-up. Trust *me*—I'll protect you."

"I know you will," Lucie said. "I believe you."

Thwock!

"And you, Elsebeth," Rudi said. "Do you believe me?"

She gripped his hand with surprising strength for one so small. "If we get lost again, you'll come for us, like you did last night?"

"I promise."

"No matter what happens?"

Rudi returned her solemn gaze. "I will go anywhere to bring you back. I will fight anyone who tries to harm you. I always will."

She smiled. "Then I believe you too."

Rudi rose out of his crouch, still holding their hands. "Let's go, then." They walked into the sun and across the meadow to the tiny house.

Hempel swung his ax at another log. *Thwock!* The log was cleaved in two, and half tumbled through the air in their direction, landing in the grass with a muffled thump. Hempel turned to retrieve it, and his gaze fell on Rudi and the girls. There was a look in his eye that Rudi had come to know well: a vacant, befuddled expression. It had appeared more and more frequently in the two years since Agnes had become his wife. Perhaps it was the way that Hempel escaped her glaring eye and sharp tongue.

"Oh!" Hempel cried, taking an awkward step back. He dropped the ax, and his hands flew up and slapped the sides of his face. His mouth formed a gaping oval.

"Hello, Uncle," Rudi said in a low, flat voice.

"Isn't that a thing! Oh, children, I'm so happy to see you all," Hempel cried, rushing to them. He lifted the girls, one in each powerful arm, and kissed them on their cheeks, then threw his arms around Rudi and lifted him as well. The grim expression on Rudi's face never changed, and he didn't return the embrace.

"Oh, Rudi, what was I thinking?" he moaned after he lowered Rudi to the ground again.

You weren't thinking at all, Rudi thought, struggling to contain the anger that flared white-hot inside him. He turned at the sound of Agnes's voice as she stepped out of the house and called to Hempel. In her hands was a wooden box that Rudi recognized at once.

"You should take these to the fair and sell them," Agnes said. "They might bring us some coin. . . ." Her voice trailed off and her eyes widened when she saw Rudi and the girls.

Only a few items peeked out of the top of the box, but that was enough to show Rudi what it contained. It held all the wooden toys he'd ever carved for himself and the girls—dolls and soldiers, wheeled horses and bears and wagons. She was selling every trace of their existence, not a day after she'd left the girls in the woods. Rudi stared at her with his mouth agape.

Agnes was caught off guard for a moment by the sight of the children. But the cold glint that was native to her eye returned soon enough. "So you're back, are you?

23

Well, what are you staring at? I'm tired of tripping over your useless toys."

Rudi glared at the face he hated so much. People who didn't know better thought that Agnes was beautiful—the men in the village were always staring and finding reasons to walk past her—but he cursed the day she'd ever met his uncle. He squeezed his hands into fists. Somehow that made it easier to hold his courage and look her in the eye. He stepped closer and lowered his voice so only she could hear him. *Don't talk to her like a boy*, he urged himself. *Talk to her like a grown-up.*

"Listen, Aunt Agnes. As soon as I possibly can, I'll take the girls with me and leave. I don't know when. Soon, I hope. But until we go, you'd better not mistreat the girls or try to lose them again."

Agnes's lip arched a little on one side. "And what makes you think you can tell me what to do, little man?"

"Just leave us alone," Rudi said. "Unless you want the whole village to know what you've done. And believe me, I'll tell them." He saw, with some satisfaction, her knuckles turn white as her fingers clenched the box. If Agnes had a soft spot, he'd just struck it: her reputation. Nobody in the village knew how cruelly she reigned at this little house down the road.

She grunted and threw the box at Rudi. He tried to catch it, but the toys tumbled out, and some of the delicate carvings broke on the ground. A red rage clouded his mind. He wanted to scream at her, but couldn't find the right words to spit out.

And that was when the voice of a stranger piped up behind him: "Oh—you dropped your things! Here, let me help you."

Neither Rudi nor Agnes had noticed him coming. Neither did Hempel and the girls, for they stared at him too, wondering who he was. The newcomer was not a young man, but he was not yet old, either. In most every way he seemed unremarkable. He was of average height and build, though better fed than most, judging by the plump roll around his waist. His hair hung straight and long on both sides of his face, like a parted curtain, and was half brown and half gray. He offered an innocent smile, but when he looked at Rudi his eyebrows flicked up, a nearly unseen gesture that hinted of conspiracy. The stranger swung his fat pack off one shoulder and laid it on the ground, so that he could bend more easily to pick up the scattered toys.

"How nice these are," he said, admiring a wooden doll. "Did someone here carve them? You, perhaps, young man?"

Rudi nodded.

"A talented hand." The stranger turned toward Hempel, who was still sweating from his work. "They say wood warms us twice," he said to Hempel. "Once when we cut it, and again when we burn it."

Hempel's eyes crossed as he concentrated. "I don't understand," he finally said.

The stranger blinked at Rudi's uncle and then gave his head a little shake. He turned to Agnes, concluding that perhaps she was the one in charge.

"My name is Horst," he said. "And I have a favor to ask. I need a place to stay."

"This is no inn," Agnes snapped, smoothing the front of her dress. "The village is a few miles down the road. You must have passed it on the way."

"Of course, dear lady," Horst said. Now his happy expression seemed a trifle pained around the eyes. "But I stayed in the village inn last night. Now I wish to stay near this part of the forest."

"The forest? Why?"

"I am mapping its borders. Do you know that no such map exists? Nobody really knows how large the forest is. Isn't that curious?"

"Not to me." Agnes sniffed. She turned to enter the house.

"I'll pay," Horst sang after her. He shook a pouch that he'd taken from his pocket, and the muffled jangle of coins called out to Agnes.

She peered back at him over one shoulder. "How much?"

Horst reached into the bag and pulled out a handful of coins. "Seven pfennigs for a week. And you must feed me as well as give me a place to sleep."

Rudi watched her stare at the silver coins. She was like a cat that just saw a bird land on its windowsill. He rolled his eyes. "Not enough," Agnes scoffed and continued into the house.

"Dear woman," Horst called out, "I think we both know my offer is generous. This is a humble house, and you are humble folk. Can you really afford to turn me away?"

Agnes's face reappeared at the window. "Very well. You can take *his* bed," she said, jabbing her finger toward Rudi. Then she was gone.

"What a lovely woman," Horst said to Rudi, smiling. "Your mother?"

"She's the mother of many things, but not children," Rudi replied.

"I see. I see very well," said Horst, chuckling. "Clever boy. Tell me, do you spend a lot of time in this forest?"

"Sure," Rudi said. "I gather wood in there all the time. That's what Uncle and I do."

"Well then. After I get myself settled, let us take a walk. I have questions, and something tells me you may have the answers."

Horst and Rudi strolled along the edge of the forest while the girls trailed behind and plucked wildflowers. Lucie had a knack for braiding flowers together into necklaces and chains, and each of them already had a crown of blossoms on her head. Rudi wondered how they could still enjoy themselves this way after the terrible thing that Aunt Agnes had done.

"You said you're mapping this forest?" he asked Horst.

"That's right," Horst said. He squinted into the dense trees.

"Who wants it mapped?"

"A wealthy and powerful man from the land where I live."

"Really? What land is that?"

Horst smiled crookedly down at Rudi. "Hold on. I'm the one with the questions. There's a landmark I'm keen to locate. Perhaps you've heard of it: a cottage, deep in the woods. It's said that a witch once lived there."

Rudi narrowed one blue eye. "Are you making fun of me?"

"What? No, of course not. Why would you say—"

"You think I'm a silly country boy who believes that story?"

"And what story would that be?" Horst asked, scratching the back of his neck.

Rudi pointed at the little house across the meadow. "Two children lived here. Hansel and Gretel. That was a long time ago—thirty or forty years, I guess. They were my father's cousins, or something like that. But anyway, there's this story that people tell . . . It's kind of weird. I don't think I really believe it."

Horst sat and patted the ground beside him. "Tell me what you've heard."

Rudi sat with his back against a large stone and his legs crossed. "When Hansel and Gretel were very young, their parents abandoned them in the forest. They were gone for weeks, and everybody was sure they were dead. But then one day they walked out of the woods and told this crazy story about what had happened to them."

Horst waved his hand in a little circle, telling Rudi to go on.

"They said that when they realized their parents weren't coming back for them, they tried to find their way back," Rudi said. "But they got lost and wandered around in the woods. And then they saw a white bird, and the bird flew ahead of them, like it was leading them somewhere. Then . . . well, you're going to think this is silly."

"The white bird led them to a cottage. A cottage made of gingerbread and candy."

Rudi stared back. "You know this story."

"I'm sure I do. Tell me if this is how it goes: They were captured by the witch who lived in the cottage, and the witch wanted to eat Hansel, but clever Gretel pushed her into her own oven."

"That's right. And Hansel and Gretel filled their pockets with as much of the witch's treasure as they could carry, and found their way home."

Horst pulled a long strand of grass from the ground and wound it around his finger, nodding to himself.

"That's a strange tale, all right. So what happened to those two? Are they still around?"

"No. My dad—he and my mom died a few years ago, and then I moved in with Uncle Hempel—my dad used to say that once Hansel and Gretel were rich with the witch's jewels, they couldn't get away from these woods fast enough. Bad memories, I guess. So they moved to some faraway land. You know, so they could 'live happily until the end of their days.'"

"'Live happily until the end of their days?'" Horst laughed. "Now you're silly. Nobody does that."

"Nobody?"

Horst leaned back and stared at the late afternoon sky. "I've heard that phrase end many a story, Rudi. If it was me, I'd write: 'And they lived as happily as could be expected, under the circumstances.'"

There was a quiet in the field, broken only by the buzz and chirp of summer insects.

"Rudi," Horst said, propping himself on one elbow, "what if *your* pockets were stuffed with the witch's treasure? What would you do?"

Rudi stared at the house again. Agnes was outside now, watching them with one hand shielding her eyes from the sun. *It must drive her mad wondering what we're talking about*, Rudi thought with great satisfaction. "I'd take the girls and get out of here. With a quick stop to say 'good riddance' to Aunt Agnes," he replied.

"What's the trouble with your aunt?"

"You know that part of the story where the grown-ups abandon Hansel and Gretel in the woods? You could say it runs in the family."

Horst's mouth dropped open. He followed Rudi's glance toward the house, where Agnes stood. "So that's what you were arguing about when I arrived. It's . . . it's hard to believe."

"Not if you know Aunt Agnes."

"But . . . what about your uncle? He didn't object?"

Rudi shrugged. "Uncle Hempel can be talked into anything. At least, he's been that way ever since Agnes showed up. He was never very bright, but he wasn't a bad man. Now it's like . . . I don't know, like he's in a fog most of the time. He just does whatever she tells him."

"And when did Agnes show up?"

"She came to the village a few years ago. She took one look at Hempel and decided he was the man for her. And I suppose he is. They go together like a hammer and a nail. What's funny is, people in the village couldn't understand why she chose Hempel. They said she was pretty enough to have any man she wanted. Those men don't know how lucky they really are."

Horst smiled. "Now, the girls, they're not your sisters?"

"No. There was a bad fire in the village, and their parents died. They had nowhere to go, and Agnes offered to take them in."

"Take them in? But she just tried to . . ."

"There was an inheritance. Not a big one, but enough

of a lure for Agnes. Of course, just a month later she was complaining that there were too many mouths to feed."

Horst looked across the meadow, and his mouth twisted. "We shouldn't have said her name aloud. Now we've summoned her, like a demon." And sure enough, Agnes was coming at them with her legs knifing through the tall grass.

"Before she gets here, Rudi, I want to ask you something," Horst said. He leaned close and spoke quickly. "Just how well do you know these woods?"

"Better than most. But they're awfully big."

"For certain. But have you seen that witch's cottage or any house at all, deep in the forest?"

Rudi laughed. "No. And believe me, other people have tried to find it, in case some of those jewels were left behind."

"Some were, Rudi," Horst said, in a low and serious tone that Rudi hadn't heard from him before. "More were left behind than were brought out."

Horst stood and Rudi did likewise. "How do you know that?" Rudi whispered.

"I simply do," Horst said, smiling slyly and glancing at Agnes. She bore down on them like a charging bull and was almost close enough to hear their words. "Quickly now, here is my offer: If you can help me find that house, you can have a fair share of any treasure we find. Then you and the girls can leave here for good. Don't answer just yet! Think about it, and tell me tonight after dinner."

CHAPTER 3

Although Horst had paid a handsome sum to lodge in the little house, the dinner was meager. Agnes spent the time shrieking at the children for mistakes that only she perceived. As soon as it could be done politely, Horst wandered outside into the dark night. Rudi helped the girls clear the table and then slipped outside when his aunt's back was turned. Horst was on the bench just outside the door, with an apple that he must have brought with him and kept in his pocket.

"What a lovely voice your aunt has," he said, crunching into the apple. "Like a cooing dove."

"Or a suit of armor rolling down stairs," Rudi said. He was still hungry, and he had to look away from the apple so his mouth wouldn't water.

"Follow me," Horst said in a low voice. He rose and paced off some distance between them and the house. "Your aunt was by the window."

Rudi laughed ruefully. "I hope she heard us." He

cleared his throat. He was used to negotiating with villagers over the price of wood; he'd been better at it than his uncle since he was ten years old. This conversation was going to be a lot like that, he thought. It was time to haggle. "So . . . you said if I help you find the witch's house, I'd get my fair share of the treasure."

"That's right," Horst said through a mouthful of apple.

Rudi crossed his arms. "Well, what's a fair share?"

Horst swallowed and grinned widely. "You get right to business, don't you, boy? So be it. I'm prepared to give you a quarter of what we find. Trust me, that will be enough to buy your farewell to Agnes."

Rudi clasped his hands behind his back and kicked at the grass with one foot. "There's something else. If we find the treasure, you have to take us with you. The girls and me. I don't even care where you're going, as long as it's far from here."

Horst looked pale at the thought. "Take you along? I don't think I'd make much of a father."

Rudi waved his hand. "No, not like that. Just get us out of here. Then we'll take care of ourselves. We'll be rich, won't we?"

"That you will. If we find the witch's cottage."

"Well—about that. There's one complication. What would you say if I told you that we'll need someone else's help to find it?"

Horst brought the apple to his mouth for another bite. "I'd say I'm talking to the wrong person."

"Then I'd say you won't find that person except through me."

"Then I'd say you can pay this person out of your share."

"Then I'd say good luck finding the cottage without us."

Horst wasn't amused anymore. "Enough. What do you propose?"

"A quarter of the treasure isn't enough. I think half should be yours. The other half is for me and the one who helps me."

"*Half?*" Horst pondered this until he'd gnawed his apple to the core. "Fine. But I get first choice of the jewels that we find. We must be clear on that. First choice is mine."

Rudi shrugged. "I don't care about that."

Horst spat an apple seed over Rudi's shoulder. "You're a brash little fellow, you know that, Rudi? What are you, twelve or thirteen years old? You ought to respect your elders better."

Rudi stared back at the house. "Well, maybe my elders haven't deserved it."

"If you say so." Horst worked his jaw from side to side, as if wondering what to say next. "You know, I'm not sure I like you much, Rudi. You've got a quick mind, but it's that mouth you should worry about. You're far too rude for a boy your age. I think whoever named you must have been a prophet. Want some advice?"

Rudi shrugged.

Horst scowled. "Watch yourself. Or that mouth will earn you a mighty wallop some day."

"From you?" Rudi said, raising one eyebrow.

"Oh, no. I'm not the hitting type. But never mind. Here's the plan. At first light, I'll go to town and buy enough food to last us a week. You meet me here with your *friend*, whoever that may be."

"Fair enough," Rudi said. He knew it wouldn't proceed exactly like that. But he didn't want to give Horst the chance to object. Tomorrow morning, of course, Horst would have no choice.

Sleep did not come easily that night. Perhaps because his aunt had given his bed to Horst, and he had to lie on an itchy mat of straw in the kitchen. Or perhaps because of the exciting possibility that had suddenly presented itself—a miracle, really, if it somehow came to be. But there was something else, some foreign thing deep in the core of his being that kept sleep at bay.

An anger had been born inside him now, a boundless rage. It was like a fire in his gut, a fire that could flare up at any moment, out of control. Why else would he lash out at Horst that way, so insolent and rude? He hoped this fury would die in time, but it didn't feel that way now; it burned low and steady in this quiet hour, ready to turn into an inferno the moment it was stoked by another outrage, another slight, another insult.

Make it stop, he told himself. With his eyes closed, he imagined a burning candle that he blew out with a puff of breath. But as he drifted off at last, and his final conscious thought turned into the first inkling of his dreams, the wick smoldered, sparked, and burst into flame again.

They stood in the meadow between the forest and the woodcutter's house. It was just past sunrise, and there was an angry blush of red in both the easterly clouds and Horst's face.

"This is not what we agreed on!"

"I know, Horst," Rudi replied. "But this is how it has to be."

Horst looked at the girls, who smiled cheerily back at him. Lucie waved with her tiny fingers. He lowered his voice to a whisper. "Rudi, we can't bring them. It might be dangerous in those woods."

"Can't be worse than in that house."

"But . . . they could stay with someone else while we're gone. Aren't there neighbors? Someone you trust?"

"Neighbors, yes. Someone I trust, no."

Horst's bottom lip flapped as he let out a long, weary breath of air. "I guess there's no choice. So where's this other fellow who knows the way?"

"It's not a fellow. And we'll meet her later. In there." Rudi pointed at the forest.

"Her?" cried Elsebeth. "Are we going to see Marusch again?" Lucie squealed with delight.

Rudi put a finger to his lips. "Quiet, girls! You'll wake my aunt. And yes, we'll see Marusch again. At least we'll try."

"What do you mean, *try?*" Horst asked.

Before Rudi could answer, the door to the house creaked open. Agnes stepped out in her nightshirt with a blanket draped over her shoulders. "You, there!" she called out, squinting through the gloom. "What are you up to?"

"Let's go," Rudi said. He put his arms around the girls' shoulders and steered them toward the forest path. Horst hesitated.

"Come on, Horst," Rudi urged.

"Don't you walk away from me," Agnes screamed.

Rudi felt that anger boil in him again. It piped up his spine and into his brain. He couldn't stop himself from turning and shouting. "What now, Aunt Agnes? First you try to get rid of the girls. Now you won't let us walk away?"

Agnes called back through the open door. "Hempel! Hempel, you oaf, come here!" But by the time Hempel stumbled sleepily out of the doorway, rubbing his eyes with both hands, Rudi and the others had disappeared into the forest.

"If you were going to change the plans, you could have let me know," Horst called forward, over the girls' heads.

"Don't worry. This'll work out all right," Rudi called back, doubting the words even as he spoke them. *All right, if I can find Marusch again. And if she'll help us.* Marusch had made it clear that she wanted to be left alone. But Rudi had no choice—this was their chance to get away from Agnes for good. He hoped Marusch would understand.

That was one concern. The other, he didn't really want to think about: the possibility of running into those strange gurgling creatures, whatever they were. He didn't want to see the faces that went with that terrible sound. He spent the next few miles peering into the shadowy places among the trees.

Rudi shivered; he was scaring himself. To better occupy his mind, he considered the names of the trees along the path and the uses for their wood. There was a crab apple; its wood was good for smoking fish. There was a beech; its wood was for boats, and a mattress stuffed with its leaves kept the bugs away. There was an elm, the choice for butcher blocks and bridges and coffins. And there was a great oak, practical for all kinds of carpentry and furniture making.

"Look, Rudi, look!" Lucie cried, pointing.

Rudi saw the boulder he'd asked them to remember: big and round, striped with quartz, and cracked like an egg. "Good eye, Lucie," he said.

"I saw it too," Elsebeth grumbled.

Rudi shrugged off his heavy pack and laid it on the ground. Horst took a sideways look at the stone. "And this has some significance?"

"Yes," Rudi said. "Girls, stay here with Horst. I'll be right back." Elsebeth was already busy pulling some woody vines out of the low branches of the trees, while Lucie plucked flowers.

Horst had his own pack off now, and tilted his head left and right to stretch his aching neck. "Hold on—where are you going?"

"Up there, to have a look around," Rudi said, examining one of the tall, long-needled evergreens that grew nearby. Its sturdy, level branches stuck out at regular heights with only a few feet between one and the next, and so it was almost as easy to climb as a ladder. Soon his hands were sticky and blackened with sap. A minute later he rose above the tops of the neighboring trees. He climbed until the branches thinned and saw before him the swaying peaks of oaks, elms, birches, maples, pines, and poplars. Back in the direction they'd come, he could see the hills and fields beyond the forest's edge. But to the north, the forest went on and on, a rolling, heaving, sweeping vista of green, until it was obscured by a low-hanging fog. He hoped the haze didn't mean that rain would come their way.

Despite Marusch's efforts to confuse them as she'd led them through the forest, Rudi had a reasonable notion of where her home lay. A smile spread across his face as he spied, some distance away, the very thing he'd hoped to see. "If you didn't want to be found, you shouldn't have put your house in the tallest tree for miles around," he said quietly, eyeing the tall, broad pine with its silvery bark.

When he climbed down, Horst was chewing

absently on a strip of salted beef. The girls sat cross-legged on a blanket, with their heads nearly touching, over something that lay between them and occupied their tiny hands.

"What do you have there?" Rudi asked them, wiping his palms on his pants in a futile effort to clean the sticky sap. Elsebeth held up the wreath that she'd made by coiling the vines and weaving flowers among them.

"Lovely," Horst said, not sounding like he meant it. "So when do we meet this lady friend of yours?"

"Pretty soon," Rudi said. He grabbed a handful of dirt and rubbed it between his palms. It made his hands filthy, but a little less sticky. Elsebeth eyed him hopefully, and he gave her a wink as he lifted his pack again and slipped his arms into the straps. "Follow me, everyone. And listen, Horst, there are some things you need to know before you meet her."

They stood underneath Marusch's tree and gazed into the branches that concealed her dwelling. "How do we know she's home?" Horst said. He looked pale at the thought of meeting the ghastly being that Rudi had described.

"We don't, really," Rudi said.

"Of course she's home," Elsebeth said knowingly. "Or the ladder would be down."

"I thought of that too," Lucie chirped.

Rudi's cheeks flushed. "Of course, Elsebeth, you're

right." He cupped his hands and called up. "Marusch! It's Rudi and the girls!"

"Hush, Rudi! She might be sleeping," Lucie said.

"She sleeps during the day, because she can't stand the sun," Elsebeth informed Horst.

Horst clutched the front of his shirt. "Can't stand the sun? Lives in a tree? What sort of creature is this!"

"A *nice* one," Lucie replied, glaring.

"*Marusch!*" Rudi shouted again.

A high, hoarse voice drifted down from the needled branches above. "You shouldn't have come."

Rudi spread his arms wide with his palms facing the sky. "I know, I know. I'm sorry. But we need your help."

"I told you not to come back. And you came back. I told you not to tell anyone about me. Yet you brought another stranger." Horst flinched and looked anxiously at Rudi.

"Marusch, please," Rudi pleaded. "We're here because we need you. But we also have an opportunity for you. It could make you rich!"

The voice from above grew cold and angry. "What good is wealth to me? Solitude is the only reward I seek, and you've robbed me of that. Be gone!"

Rudi punched his open palm. Was everyone older than he put on earth just to throw obstacles in his path? He took a step back and raised his voice. "Listen, Marusch! We're not leaving. How would you like it if we went back and told the whole village about you?"

There was a *twang* from above, and suddenly an arrow wobbled in the ground at Rudi's feet. Horst yelped, and ran behind a nearby tree.

The voice came again. "And how would you like to be hunted down like a rabbit before you ever got back to your accursed village?"

"Oh, Rudi," Elsebeth groused. She stepped into the open, pulling Lucie behind her, and turned her face toward the voice in the trees. "Please, Marusch. Don't be mad at Rudi—he's not always this horrible. We would so like to see you again. Look what we've made you!" Lucie held the wreath high.

There was no answer for what seemed like a minute. Then the ladder tumbled down, uncoiling as it fell. Elsebeth smiled tartly at Rudi.

"Thank you, girls," Rudi said softly. He felt like banging his head against the tree to punish himself after letting his temper get the best of him again. Marusch probably hated him now. "You go up first, Elsie and Lucie. I'll be right behind you." He called over his shoulder, "Come on, Horst."

Horst leaned out from behind a tree. "What, you expect me to climb that?"

When Rudi reached Marusch's house, the girls were already by her side, hugging her. Marusch's brow furrowed when she saw him.

"I'm sorry," Rudi said. "It was terrible to threaten you like that. I hope you know, I'd never tell anyone about you."

"You already have," Marusch said, looking at the hand that clumsily shoved a pack up through the hole in the floor. She pulled the hood of her cloak over her head and turned away.

"Somebody—help me before I fall," Horst pleaded. Rudi grabbed him by the wrist and hauled him up. Horst slumped to the floor and gasped like a fish. Finally he saw Marusch standing with her back to them. He glanced at Rudi, stood and brushed himself off.

"Marusch," Rudi said quietly, "this is Horst. He's a mapmaker from far away."

"What does a mapmaker want with me?" Marusch said without turning.

Horst wiped his sweaty palms on his shirt. "Not to reveal your whereabouts, good lady. Never that. For now, I only wish to thank you for letting me visit. May I?"

Slowly Marusch turned, keeping her head bowed. Horst took her hand and kissed it, then pressed his other hand on top of hers. Rudi watched carefully, and as Marusch slowly raised her head and revealed her terrible white face with the shrunken lips and crimson-stained teeth, Horst never flinched; his smile and gaze were steady. "Thank you, Marusch. It is my pleasure to meet you. May we sit and talk for a while?"

Rudi sighed quietly. From one minute to the next, he wasn't sure how he felt about Horst, but at that moment, he admired him very much indeed.

If Marusch was pleased or impressed by the gesture, Rudi couldn't tell. She merely left the little room, pushing aside the hide that covered the doorway, and walked onto her covered porch.

Horst stared at the gently swinging skin. "Does she want us to follow her?"

"I guess," Rudi said. He gestured for the girls to stay inside, and he and Horst followed Marusch. She was sitting on the floor of the porch, apparently waiting for them, and they did the same.

"Well?" she asked.

"Rudi, why don't you tell her why we've come," said Horst. "And let me unpack some things." While Rudi explained what had happened since Marusch guided them home, Horst burrowed into his pack and produced biscuits and shortbread and carrots and plums, jars of honey and jam, and a box of sweets that made Rudi's mouth water to look at them. Marusch's eyes widened, and she stared at the goods all the while. Horst interrupted Rudi's story to call to the girls, and when Lucie and Elsebeth came out he filled their cupped hands with sweets, then sent them back inside with enormous smiles lighting up their faces.

Marusch sampled everything that Horst brought, closing her eyes and nodding as she swallowed. Rudi supposed that these tastes hadn't crossed her tongue in many a year. He went on with his story, not even sure if she was paying attention. But when he reached the part about the cottage in the forest, she suddenly looked up and stared at him.

"You've seen it!" Horst said with an eager smile.

Marusch shrugged. "I've seen a cottage, deep in the woods. A day's journey north. I lived closer to there once. Before I had to move, and came here."

"Tell me what it looks like," Horst said, leaning forward.

"I was only there a few times," Marusch said. She looked out one of the windows, as if the distant place could be seen from there. "It was small. Not much larger than this house. With a tiny stable nearby . . ."

"Yes," Horst whispered.

"Three rooms inside," Marusch said. "It was furnished once, but everything was smashed to pieces." *By who?* Rudi wondered.

Marusch rubbed her temples. "But in the kitchen, still standing, there was a tall chimney and an enormous stove of iron, with a door this wide." She held her hands as far apart as her shoulders.

Horst slapped his knees and clasped his hands together. "Ha! That's it! The witch's house! You were right, Rudi, Marusch was the one to ask!"

Rudi nodded. "But Marusch, why'd you have to move your home?"

Marusch had a nearly empty jar of jam in her hands. She ran a finger inside, licked it clean, and placed the jar carefully on the floor before she answered. "Something was in the forest, to the north. A waxing darkness. An evil I could smell in the air and taste in the water. Strange creatures began to prowl about, closer and closer to my home. And I was not a tree dweller in those days—I was vulnerable."

Rudi felt a chill creep up his back like a spider. "Creatures—you mean like the ones you and I heard?" Marusch nodded.

"What creatures?" Horst said, stiffening. "You never said a thing about creatures!"

Rudi shrugged. "Sorry, Horst. It didn't seem important at the time. But Marusch, when did those things start showing up around here?"

"Only these past few weeks. Perhaps a month. This darkness spreads, like an infection."

Rudi pondered this for a while. Marusch devoured another pastry. And Horst grumbled, "You should have told me about the creatures."

"Look," Rudi said, "the important thing is that she knows where the house is. Marusch, would you lead us there?"

She leaned back against the railing and crossed her arms. "Why should I help a boy who won't keep his word?"

Rudi groaned. "I know. I promised we'd leave you alone. But you're the only one who can help us. Horst says there's a fortune in jewels in that cottage, waiting to be found. I need that fortune, Marusch, so I can take Lucie and Elsebeth away and keep them safe."

Just then an explosion of girlish giggles came from

inside the house. Marusch turned toward the sound. Her head inclined a little, and her shoulders sagged.

"Even if I showed you the way, there is no fortune there," she said.

Rudi's heart twisted at these words, but Horst smiled and waved his hand as if shooing a fly. "Don't worry, Rudi," he said, "she wouldn't have known where to look."

"And how is it that *you* know?" Marusch said. Rudi was getting used to her face, and he found that he could begin to read her subtle expressions. Now one of her eyebrows was raised slightly as she stared at Horst; this was suspicion.

"I'm sorry, but how I came by that knowledge is my business for now," Horst replied.

Rudi leaned toward her and pleaded with his eyes. "But you'll help us, Marusch? Please?"

Marusch paused for what seemed like an eternity. A pinecone fell from the branches above and clattered on the porch. Finally she spoke. "You must have addled my brain with these sweets and jams. Yes, I will help you. But not for you, Rudi. Or this mapmaker. I will do it for the girls. It's not their fault you ignored my request."

Horst struggled to keep his mouth from grinning. "So, shall we all set out tomorrow?"

Marusch had chosen a plum to eat. She cupped it in both hands, closed her eyes and brought it to her nose for a deep sniff. Rudi could see her ghastly mouth change shape—the shrunken lips pulled back even farther and the cheekbones rose. *That's her smile,* he realized.

She took a deep bite, chewed rapturously, and turned at last to answer Horst. "No," she said.

"*No?* What do you mean, 'no'?" Horst shot an anxious glance at Rudi.

"We can't all go," she said, lowering her voice. "I won't lead the girls into peril."

"Then leave them here—they'll be fine," Horst replied.

"Six and seven years old, and alone for two days?" Rudi cried. "We can't do that! But Marusch, could Horst and I find our way there if you told us how?"

Marusch nodded. "I will take you part of the way. But I have warned you—it may be dangerous."

"It's worth the risk," Horst said flatly. He gazed in the direction where he imagined the cottage lay.

Rudi thought about his aunt and uncle, what they'd tried to do to the girls, and their miserable house by the forest's edge. *No doubt,* he thought. *It's worth the risk.*

CHAPTER 4

The first notion of daylight had just occurred to the sky when Marusch woke them.

"So, you are a maker of maps?" she asked Horst.

"That's right," Horst said through a yawn. He grimaced and arched his back, stretching after an uncomfortable night on the floor.

"Have you a compass?"

"A what? Oh, a compass—no, I'm afraid I do not."

Marusch raised one eyebrow at Horst, then walked around to the other side of the tree trunk that passed through the room like a column. Rudi heard her open and shut the lid of her wooden chest, and then she returned with a small, nearly flat box in the palm of her hand. She passed it to Horst, who opened the lid. Inside were a shallow brass dish, a long thick needle, and a tiny piece of cork. Horst looked at it, puzzled.

"It's my compass, *mapmaker*," Marusch said. "You will need it when we part company. Just fill the dish with water and balance the needle on the cork. The narrow end will turn north."

"A compass, of course," Horst said. "Forgive me, I'm still half asleep."

Rudi looked back one last time at the tree, and heard Lucie and Elsebeth call good-bye from the hidden house. "Come back soon!" Elsebeth cried.

He hated to leave them behind. *But I'll be back in two days,* he promised himself. *And our lives will be changed forever.*

Marusch led them to a stream, and they followed it, walking against its current along the bank. Her hood was up and the stained glass shielded her eyes from the rising sun. After some miles, she allowed Horst to take the lead, and then tugged on Rudi's sleeve to slow him.

"Be careful with this man," she whispered.

"Horst? Why?"

"What sort of mapmaker has no compass?" she asked. And then Horst realized that the distance between them had grown, and he stopped to wait.

They reached a place where the stream flowed over a rock ledge and splashed into a deep pool before meandering again on its way. Marusch filled the brass dish with water and set the needle on the floating cork. She placed the compass in Rudi's hand, and he watched the needle swerve and point across the stream. It never stopped entirely, but wagged back and forth like a dog's tail.

"That is the way," Marusch said. "Directly north. When the shadows grow long, you will find another stream, narrower and swifter than this one, which flows to the west. Follow its current, and within an hour you will reach the cottage. You can make it before sunset, if you hasten. I trust you can find your way back."

"Many thanks, Marusch," Horst said.

"Yes. Thank you." Rudi said, looking into the blue glass that masked her eyes. She gave him a slow nod, full of meaning. Then she turned and moved swiftly back down the stream. Rudi noticed that her habit was to step on rocks and fallen limbs whenever possible, so she would leave no trail.

Rudi led the way across the stream, stepping nimbly from stone to stone. Horst followed, slower and clumsier, using a stick he'd found to keep his balance. They plunged deeper and deeper into the woods, and consulted the needle every few miles to keep their course true.

"Do you suppose there are bears around here? Or wolves?" Horst said, in a higher pitch than usual.

Rudi smiled, knowing Horst couldn't see his face from behind. "Bears and wolves? In a forest? I suppose it's possible."

"Don't mock me, Rudi. I've lived in a city nearly all my life. I'm just . . . out of my element in these woods."

Rudi felt a pang of remorse. Then he heard something in the woods to their right—thumping steps, coming closer. Horst screamed as a large stag bounded out from between two trees. It had a tan hide, slender legs, and broad thorny antlers. The handsome beast fixed one dark brown eye on them as it soared across their path. The stag turned gracefully in the air and touched the ground for an instant with its front and back hooves paired. It sprang off at a new angle, and flew through the air in a long, graceful arc. An instant later it vanished again, and the tromp of its feet faded to silence.

Horst leaned against a tree with one hand over his heart and laughed at himself.

"I was about to say I'm sorry," Rudi said, laughing with him.

Horst took a long moment to recover. "Oh, never mind about that. If I was you, with a muttonhead for an uncle and a viper for an aunt, I'd probably be a disrespectful little whelp too." He stood and shifted his pack on his shoulders. "Go on, lead the way, Rudi. I've never felt so lost. I'm useless in these woods."

People like Horst, who'd never spent much time in the forest, always assumed that it looked the same no matter how far in you went: just trees and trees and more trees. But people like Rudi, who'd spent much of their lives exploring it, knew the forest was ever changing.

As they walked along now, the trees first grew older

and fatter and taller, until a dense ceiling of a thousand shades of green blotted out most of the sky. Only a few bright dapples of light reached the ground, and they shifted and winked as a breeze that could not be felt on the forest floor ruffled the treetops a hundred feet above. Then they passed into a region where bristling evergreens ruled, and the countless needles they had shed over the years formed a brown mat that poisoned the ground for all but a few hardy weeds. And then came a blackened world, where regal trees had once towered before a fire cast them down decades before. Now vigorous saplings lofted over the ferns and charred stumps in a race for sunlight that many years from now only a few would win and then spread their branches wide to cast their brothers into shade and slow starvation. Then the landscape altered again, and they were in a dank place where brown, knobby-knuckled vines snaked through the branches of the trees.

On another day Rudi might have seized a vine and swung with a whoop across the forest floor. But not on this day, with such an important task ahead. And maybe never again. Since he'd raced into the woods to find Lucie and Elsebeth, it seemed like the carefree urges to which he'd once surrendered happily had been left in ashes, burned away by the anger that he could still feel, hot as coals in the pit of his soul.

The ground under their feet changed as well. Sometimes they walked on springy moss, and sometimes they stumbled across roots that intertwined like petrified serpents. Twice they found themselves before a body of water: once a cheerful lake that glittered under the sun, and once a lonely pond that rested still and dark under the shadows of encroaching trees, ripples spreading only when something unseen touched its surface from below.

They paused only to eat, or when Horst needed to rest. He took one long break, leaning against a tree with his eyes closed. Rudi stared at him and thought about Marusch's warning. "Horst?" he called.

"Hmm?" Horst replied, without opening his eyes or mouth.

"Will you tell me how you learned about the jewels?"

Horst stretched, leaned forward, and put his elbows on his knees. "Rudi . . . I've been looking for the right time to tell you something. I might as well do it now." He scratched the back of his neck and grinned sheepishly. "I'm not a mapmaker."

Rudi scowled. "I kind of figured."

"And I'm not Horst, either."

Liar, Rudi thought. His familiar anger flared again. "Then who are you?"

"My name is Hansel."

CHAPTER 5

"*H*ansel? Not the Hansel who . . ." Rudi couldn't finish the sentence.

"Yes. That Hansel." He stood and arranged his pack over his shoulders once more. "Why don't we get moving? I'll tell you more while we walk. What does the compass say?"

Rudi filled the bowl with water once again and floated the needle. "This way," he said, practically growling. He stomped off at a brisk pace, kicking dead branches out of his way.

Hansel hurried to catch up. "Slow down! What are you so furious about? I thought you'd be happy that I confided in you. You wouldn't act like this if you saw things from my perspective."

"What perspective is that?" Rudi called over his shoulder. There was a slender branch across his path; he pushed it away and let it snap back behind him to lash Hansel across the chest.

"I couldn't just—ouch! Curse you, boy, did you do that on purpose? I couldn't just walk into your village and announce that the famous Hansel was back to collect the rest of the witch's treasures, could I? And when I got to your house and overheard that harpy Agnes, I decided to wear the mask a little longer. Wouldn't you have done the same?"

The words made sense. Rudi supposed that yes, he would have done the very same thing. But it still hurt to be deceived. He stopped and faced Hansel. "You could have told me once we set off. I guess you didn't trust me."

Hansel raised his hands, palms out. "Fair enough. But I wanted to meet your helper first, and you were so mysterious about her. This trust thing goes both ways, you know. Then, once I met Marusch . . . well, she frightened me a little, to be honest. So I waited until you and I were alone. Look, if I tell you I trust you now, will you wipe that awful look off your face?"

Rudi gnashed his teeth. "Just don't lie to me anymore. I'm sick of lies."

Hansel rubbed his temple, as if his head ached. "Yes, Rudi. Of course, Rudi."

Later, as they walked on, a question occurred to Rudi. "So why do you need my help to find the cottage? You've already been there."

"It's been almost forty years, Rudi. I hadn't the vaguest memory of how to get back. Gretel and I wandered the forest for days before we found our way out. So I knew

I needed a guide. I asked the innkeeper at Waldrand who knew these woods best. He said a hunter named Burck—who he wouldn't recommend for company—and a woodcutter named Hempel. And wouldn't you know it, Hempel lived in the same miserable house where I grew up. I couldn't believe it was still standing. Once I got there, though, it seemed like you were a better choice than your uncle. He's a bit . . . well, you know."

Every answer raised another question. "So where's Gretel?"

Hansel's shoulders sagged. "I truly don't know. I haven't seen her since she was eighteen. She married a merchant who granted her fondest wish: to sail away, as far as possible from the very place I'm trying to find." He smiled sadly.

"And where've you been all these years?"

"If you go east from your village, around the shadow of this forest, and then far, far north, you come to a land that meets the sea, with a broad peninsula and too many islands to count. That is where we went, Gretel and Father and I. To Kurahaven: a wonderful city on the sea with princes and scholars and artists and architects and musicians. There are towers that soar into the air with swallow-tailed banners flapping at their peaks, and a bustling port where ships sail in from distant lands all day long. Gretel married, Father died, and I spent my days at the great university, to make myself a learned man."

As he listened to Hansel prattle on in his dreamy tone, Rudi suddenly felt small and unimportant, even vaguely insulted. "If it was so wonderful, why are you back?"

Hansel shrugged. "I ran out of money. I never wanted—" He stopped suddenly, because Rudi had halted before him. "What is it, Rudi?"

It was late afternoon, and their shadows had grown long. Just ahead was a stream that was smaller and swifter than the first one they followed. "We're almost there," Rudi said. They turned west and followed the course of the stream.

An hour later they saw a clearing not far from the bank. Rudi's pulse quickened as he saw, in the shade of the open space, a small cottage and a tiny stable.

"There it is," Hansel said.

"There it is," Rudi echoed.

The cottage's foundation was built of stones. Above the rock, the log walls had begun to decay. Part of the thatch of the roof had rotted away, baring the slanted timbers that met at the peak. The stone chimney stood uncorrupted, and now it rose like an ancient monument. It cast a long shadow that pointed eerily toward where they stood.

Hansel wavered and put a hand on Rudi's shoulder. When he spoke, his voice was weak. "I—I thought I could bear it. But now that I'm here . . ."

"The witch died, Hansel," Rudi said. This felt strange, having to reassure an adult. It should have been the other way around. "Gretel pushed her into the oven that was meant for you."

"I know, I know," Hansel said. He mopped the sweat off his brow with the back of his cuff. "Strange—I feel too hot and too cold, at the same time."

"We'll have to spend the night here," Rudi said. "It's the only shelter we've got."

"No!" Hansel said. "Never here. I couldn't. I'll sleep in the woods."

Rudi took a look at Hansel's quaking legs. He knew he'd have to show enough courage for both of them. "Come on, Hansel. Let's get it over with." He stepped toward the cottage. Hansel hesitated, rearranged the pack on his shoulders, and finally followed. His eyes never left the stable that had once been his prison.

The cottage door was half open. It hung from one last tenacious, rusted hinge. Rudi pushed it open the rest of the way. The hinge screeched horribly, and a pair of rats darted past him, sending Hansel into a mad dance as they skittered between his feet.

Hansel stepped inside, breathing loud and fast. Then his panting stopped altogether. Rudi looked at his face, and saw him stare at the largest object in the room: a great iron oven. Its wide door was big enough to crawl through without touching the sides, and it was partly open. The space inside looked as black and endless as the night sky.

"Ulfrida. The witch's name was Ulfrida. Did you know that?" Hansel said.

Rudi shook his head. He tried to imagine himself in Hansel's shoes, returning after so many years to the place where he'd been kept for weeks by a foul child-eating witch—returning to see the oven he'd narrowly escaped. A shiver coursed through Rudi's limbs. *Ulfrida.* He turned in a circle and looked at the smashed table and chairs and cabinets, and the shelves ripped from the walls. Rusted utensils and pans were bent and scattered across the floor. Through open doorways, he could see two other rooms, also vandalized. "Where are the jewels?" he asked.

Hansel blinked rapidly, as if awakening. With great effort, he produced a weak smile. "I think I remember," he said.

You'd better, Rudi thought.

He followed Hansel, who drifted like a sleepwalker into one of the adjoining rooms, talking quietly. "After Gretel slew the witch and freed me, we came into this, the room where Ulfrida slept. There was a chest of wood, dark with age and bound with iron."

Hansel pointed. Next to the pile of splinters, rotted fabric, and straw—an old bed, Rudi realized—he saw the remains of the chest, its dark wood smashed to pieces. "It was filled with jewels," Hansel said. "Enough to make a prince go weak in the knees. More than we could carry."

"So what did you do with the rest?"

Hansel smiled, more genuinely this time. "Gretel was

61

clever enough to trick Ulfrida. But I was the one who suggested that we hide the jewels we couldn't carry." He walked to the center of the room and stared at the floor, which was made of flat slabs of stone. Then he squatted and crooked his finger, gesturing for Rudi to come.

Rudi kneeled beside him, as Hansel pointed to the slab beneath him, and the tiny letter H that was scratched in the corner. Hansel ran his finger along the seam between that slab and the next, digging a groove in the narrow band of dirt, until he could get his fingertips under the stone and pry it up.

There was nothing but gray soil underneath.

"You're sure this was the right stone?" Rudi asked.

Hansel didn't reply. He pawed at the dirt like a dog, slinging handfuls behind him. Soon he exposed a round, flat object, black and rough, with a knob in the middle. "One of the pots from her kitchen," Hansel said. His spirits had revived, and he chuckled as he lifted the covered pot from the hole.

Rudi trembled. "Open it."

Hansel put his hand on the knob and held it there, keeping the lid on tight. He licked his lips. "Remember our agreement."

Rudi grinned. "Half is yours. And half is mine to share with Marusch."

Hansel's face grew serious. "Yes—but there was more. First choice is mine. Remember?"

"I don't care," Rudi said. "Just open it!"

Hansel filled his lungs, held his breath, and yanked the cover off the pot.

Even in the weak dusky light that came through a small window in the bedroom, the fortune inside glittered and shined. In all his life Rudi had seen only a few precious stones, on the rings and necklaces of wealthy travelers. But those gems were as small and dull as grains of sand compared to the heap of rubies, emeralds, diamonds, and sapphires inside the pot. There were dozens upon dozens, and they twinkled in every color. It looked as if someone had shattered a rainbow and gathered the shards. There were gold coins too, a hundred or more, engraved with unreadable words and the faces of unknown kings and emperors.

Rudi had been perched on his knees, but the sight made him so giddy that he toppled over and lay there laughing, thrusting his fists toward the ceiling. Hansel hooted and clapped. He turned the pot on its side and the treasure clattered onto the stone floor.

Rudi sat up and stared at the twinkling fortune. He couldn't quite believe this was happening. "What will you choose?"

Hansel studied the pile. He rubbed at his chin, and then finally reached down for a dark, crude chain. He tugged at it, and slowly drew its thick, irregular links from the pile, stirring the more lustrous objects around it. Finally, at the end of the chain, a stone emerged that was locked inside an iron cage. It was dull and ruddy, and roughly cut into a shape like an almond. *Or an eye*, Rudi thought, as he watched it swing back and forth before Hansel palmed it and stuffed chain and stone alike into his pocket.

"That's your first choice? It doesn't seem like much," Rudi said.

"True, but it's different from the rest. Makes it special somehow." Hansel drew his sleeve across his brow; he seemed to harbor an endless reservoir of perspiration. "Besides, there's plenty of fancy stuff left. And half is yours—to share as you wish!" He clapped Rudi on the back. "Why don't you pick something now?"

It was Rudi's turn to ponder. "Look at these," he said. He lifted an identical pair of silver necklaces, each holding a fat blue gemstone.

"I know what you're thinking," Hansel said. "One for each of the girls. Go on, Rudi. Take them. Then we'll stuff the rest into two sacks, and that will be it."

A few minutes later they stood, not minding the extra weight in their packs. "Feels light as a feather to me," Hansel said. "Now let's get out of here."

"Should we fix that?" Rudi asked. He pointed at the empty hole in the floor.

"What does it matter now?" Hansel replied. He stepped into the main room again and his smile faltered. He was transfixed by the stove once more. "I've seen it so many times in my dreams," he said. "Maybe now I can leave it behind forever."

Rudi allowed Hansel this last quiet moment. Then the silence was broken by a noise from the forest—a low gurgle like a murderous wet purr. Rudi wasn't certain if he'd heard it or imagined it. Then it came again, much louder. He looked at Hansel, wondering if he'd noticed it too. Hansel's face had gone white.

"What was that?" Hansel said hoarsely.

Rudi stared past the half-closed front door. He knew the sound. It was the one he'd dreaded hearing since they started this journey.

He heard the bubbling gurgle again, louder still, and this time it was joined by the rustle of leaves. Through a tiny gap in the dense trees beyond the clearing, he caught a glimpse of a shape moving toward the cottage.

"It'll see us if we go out the door," he whispered.

"*What* will see us?" Hansel whined back.

Rudi looked around. The windows were tiny, and he doubted Hansel could squeeze through. They had to hide, but every cabinet and closet was smashed. Then he saw the oven, wide and deep. "Come on," he urged, pulling Hansel by the sleeve.

Hansel's eyes blinked madly as he realized what Rudi meant to do. "No!" he mouthed.

The gurgling came again, clearer now, as if the thing had stepped into the open space where no trees muffled the sound. Rudi tugged harder, and Hansel allowed himself to be dragged into the maw of the oven. They had to hunch to make it through the opening. Rudi pulled the door closed gently. He was able to bring it within inches of shutting completely before it resisted and began to squeak.

They crouched side by side in the darkness, nearly filling the space. The cool iron walls and ceiling were oppressively close. Rudi put his fingers to the oven's floor to steady himself and felt them sink into a fine layer of ash.

He saw nothing but pale light in the narrow vertical space where the door hadn't closed entirely. Behind him, Hansel groaned. "Shhh!" Rudi said. And then he heard the tortured *scree-ee-eech* of a rusted hinge as something pushed the cottage door farther open. Hansel grabbed Rudi's forearm and squeezed.

With his senses honed by fear, Rudi heard the thing enter the cottage. Its steps sounded strange, like something flat and soggy slapping against the stone floor. The thing gurgled again, only a few feet away. It sounded like a man had filled the back of his mouth with water and let the air from his lungs bubble through it. Behind him, Rudi heard Hansel's rapid, shallow breath getting faster and louder.

Rudi saw something through the narrow gap where the oven door hadn't closed completely: a silver spearhead that narrowed to a lethal point. It glided silently by, and after it, came a long shaft made of some dark and polished wood. Then Rudi saw the hand that gripped the spear. It was so close that he could have reached out and seized it; but never would he dream of touching that strange hand with its long fingers that ended in bulbous lumps, and its slick skin the mottled color of mushrooms. Rudi only caught a glimpse of the body through the constricted space. It was the size of a man, but thinner and more sinuous.

Rudi held his breath. He was sure the hand would come back and pull the oven door open. What could he do—fight? He clenched his hands into fists, ready to jump out. But the creature moved on. Rudi let his breath out slowly and quietly through his nostrils.

The thing padded across the room, and the footsteps grew faint. Hansel's hands gripped him even harder when the next sound came—a sound that could only be the iron pot in the witch's room being knocked onto its side. Rudi heard a loud gurgle that rose in pitch, and he imagined the creature staring at the exposed hole in the floor. *We should have covered it*, he thought. *Stupid!* He hoped that, to this creature, the sight was meaningless. But that hope failed as he heard its feet slapping the floor once more, but faster now. A shadow flashed by the oven door, and a moment later the cottage door squealed again.

"I think it left," Rudi whispered a minute later. He was about to suggest that they stay in hiding a while longer to be sure, but Hansel suddenly clawed past him, grunting like a pig as he crawled on his hands and knees. Hansel flung the oven door wide, got to his feet and bolted. Rudi went after him. He didn't bother to shout and add to the noise. He followed Hansel out the cottage door, across the clearing and into the trees. It was nearly dark now, and Hansel stumbled over a tree root and fell to the ground.

Rudi put a hand under his arm and helped him up. "Slow down," he said, holding Hansel to keep him from running again, "or you'll put your face in a tree."

"Get us out, Rudi. Get us away from here!"

"Fine with me," Rudi replied. He was just as anxious to put miles between them and the cottage. "This is the right direction for now. The stream is just ahead. Come on."

They ran as swiftly as they dared in the meager light, hunched over with their hands before them to keep the branches from their eyes. Finally Hansel tugged at Rudi's shoulder, out of breath.

"Was that . . . was that one of the creatures Marusch talked about?"

"Yes," Rudi replied.

"I can't believe it showed up tonight," Hansel moaned.

"Maybe it comes *every* night." The idea gnawed at Rudi, that this thing patrolled the woods and the cottage, and the discovery of the hole in the floor had sent it rushing away. *Away to where? Away to who?*

CHAPTER 6

Rudi dug into his pack, past the heavy sack of gems and gold, and pulled out his tinderbox. It was so dark now that he could barely see Hansel beside him, so when he opened the lid he had to use his fingers to find what he needed inside: the flint, the steel, the charred linen, and the bits of dried grass and pine needles.

He spread the small patch of linen on a rock. Then he slipped his fingers through the flat ring of steel, made a fist of that hand, and struck the steel across the lump of flint. A shower of sparks, tiny flecks of white-hot steel, flew onto the blackened cloth. After a few attempts, one spark caught on the fabric and twinkled there like a red star. He lowered his face and blew on the spot. It smoldered, brightened, and then a tiny flame appeared. This he fed with dried grass and pine needles. Usually he would have stoked the flame with bits of wood, each larger than the one before, until he'd built a lively blaze. But they didn't need a fire to last the night. In fact, a bright beacon in the night would be a terrible idea.

Rudi dug into his pack and found a candle, one of the items that Hansel had bought for the excursion. He lit the wick by the flame, placed the candle in its holder, and clapped on the glass sleeve that would protect the flame from the breeze. Then he smothered the fire with dirt.

By the candle's light Rudi consulted the compass once more. Soon they headed south again, back toward Marusch's dwelling. The way was slow in the night, but every stride away from the cottage made them both feel better.

"I don't think I can take another step," Hansel said hours later.

"I think it's safe to rest," Rudi said. They unpacked blankets and cocooned themselves on mossy ground that was unexpectedly comfortable. Rudi pulled his pack, heavy with the weight of gold and gems, close to his side and looped his arm under the strap. "We did it," he said, as much to himself as Hansel. "We found it."

"Yes. But I'll feel better when I'm on the road and miles from this forest."

"Don't forget, you promised to take us with you. I want to take the girls and leave at once. Get them away from Aunt Agnes."

"That was our bargain. I'll get you away from the village, but then you're on your own. Don't expect to live with me or anything like that. I'm not the fatherly type."

"I understand. But . . . I wondered. Will you go back to your city? Your city by the sea?"

"I suppose I will."

"I'd like to see it. Could you take us all the way there? We are family, after all, you and I. Distant cousins."

"Cousins. I suppose we are. Yes, you can come along. The girls are good company. And you aren't so bad when you're not losing your temper."

Rudi pulled the pack a little closer and smiled. After a while, he called out softly. "Hansel?"

"Yes?" came Hansel's voice from the dark.

"What they say about you and Gretel. Is everything about that story true?"

"Which part do you mean?"

"Well, people say that after you escaped from the witch, you rode a great duck across the lake to get home."

"Humph. Sounds like someone's added to the story."

"And the witch's cottage. It looked like a plain house to me just now, but I heard it was made of cake and candy. . . ."

"So it seemed to Gretel and me. When we first saw it, it looked as if the walls were made of gingerbread, with sheets of sugar candy where windowpanes should have been, and icicles made of frosting. But once the witch had us, those things were gone. Suddenly it was an ordinary cottage made of stone and wood. It was all just illusion; a spell the witch cast, to make us see what wasn't there."

"I didn't know such a thing was possible."

"More things are possible than you can conceive, Rudi. Things both evil and good."

Minutes passed. "Are you sleeping, Hansel?"

"Just resting. I won't sleep until we reach Marusch's home. And maybe not even then. What is it now, Rudi?"

"That city by the sea—what did you say it was called?"

"Kurahaven," Hansel said.

Kurahaven. The name was beautiful. Rudi let it echo in his mind, and a deep happiness filled him as he thought of taking Lucie and Elsebeth to a better world far, far away, a city of towers and merchant ships and swallow-tailed banners that snapped in the ocean breeze. Sure, he was just a boy, but he could take care of the girls. They'd be rich, and money could buy them anything they needed. Even a servant. That's what he'd do—he'd pay a woman with a kind face and a good heart to take care of them all, and dress the girls in beautiful clothes. And the three of them would live as happily as could be expected.

He heard Hansel begin to snore, despite his vow, and the need to sleep came to him as well. He surrendered to it, saying the name to himself as his thoughts dimmed: *Kurahaven, Kurahaven.*

Rudi sensed the morning light through his eyelids. He rubbed the sleep from his eyes, and turned to where Hansel had slept. Hansel sat cross-legged and stared at the crude gem that he'd chosen from the pile. The chain was around his neck, and he held the little iron cage between his thumbs and forefingers. He heard Rudi stir and spoke without taking his eyes off the stone.

"Morning, little cousin. We slept longer than we meant to. Do something for me, will you? Look at those trees over there and tell me what you see."

Rudi was puzzled by the request, but he looked. "Just the trees. And a little morning mist, if that's what you mean."

Hansel frowned. "Mist? Yes. That's what I meant." He shoved the ruddy stone inside his shirt. "We should go."

"I see something now," Rudi said.

"Eh?" Hansel had turned away and bent down to stuff his blanket into his pack.

"A white bird," Rudi said. The bird had just fluttered out of the deep woods and alighted on a branch. It turned its head sideways to stare at them. Rudi had never seen one like it. It was large, the size and shape of a raven, but pure white except for its dark legs and beak and glittering, oily eyes.

Hansel straightened and turned around stiffly. All the color drained from his face as his eyes found the bird. He opened his mouth as if to speak, but only a choke came out. The white bird hopped off the limb it was on and glided to a closer, lower branch. It turned its head to stare at them again. *No*, Rudi thought, *it's not staring at us. It's staring at* him.

Hansel reached for a stick on the ground and slung it at the bird. "Get away from me!" he shrieked. The bird leaped nimbly off the branch to avoid the spinning stick and flapped off into the trees, never making a sound.

"What was that?" Rudi said, watching the bird disappear.

"*What was that?* Don't you remember?" Hansel snapped, as if accusing Rudi of something. "The white bird! The bird that led Gretel and me to the witch's cottage. We thought it would save us, but it led us to *her*!"

Rudi shook his head, open-mouthed. "All these years later? It can't be the same bird."

Hansel pulled his pack hurriedly onto his shoulders and glared at Rudi, tight-lipped and pale. "Have you ever seen a bird like that? *Ever?*"

"Well, no."

"Neither have I! Not since I was a child in these woods! Now which is the way out of here? *Hurry!*"

Many hours later Hansel called for help once more as he reached the top of the ladder to Marusch's house. Rudi and the girls seized his wrists and hauled him up until he lay gasping on the floor.

"Are you all right, Horst?" Elsebeth asked, bending over him.

"His name isn't Horst. It's Hansel," Rudi said.

"Hansel? You mean like Hansel and Gretel?" said Lucie.

Hansel didn't bother to reply. He raised his hand and waved weakly.

"A lot like that," Rudi said. "But he didn't want anyone to know he was back to find the treasure."

Marusch inclined her head curiously. "So it's Hansel. And did you find it?"

Rudi smiled. During the last miles of the journey back, he'd rehearsed this moment in his mind over and over again. He reached into his pocket, pulled out the twin necklaces, and handed one to each of the girls. Lucie and Elsebeth gasped with delight and clutched the jewels to their hearts. Then Rudi dumped the bag out onto the floor, and the girls squealed at the sight of the glittering pile.

"Half is yours," Rudi told Marusch. "For helping us find the cottage. And for saving the girls when they were lost."

Marusch was unmoved. "These are things of your world, not mine. They can do me no good."

"Please keep them, Marusch," Elsebeth said. She wrapped her arms around Marusch's waist. "You deserve something."

Marusch ran her hand across Elsebeth's hair, and Rudi saw her smile again. "It's all right, child," she said.

Rudi reached into the pile with two hands and pushed it apart. "Half is yours, and that's final."

Marusch turned toward Rudi, awkward now because Lucie too clung to her waist. "Rudi, what use are they to me? I cannot go to any village to trade them. Don't you know how people treat me, because of this face?"

"Don't say that, Marusch," Elsebeth moaned, squeezing her.

"Rudi, girls. We have to go," Hansel announced, with all the authority he could muster. He turned to Marusch. "And you should leave as well, good lady. That darkness you spoke of is real, and worse than you can imagine. I fear one day it will reach you here."

Marusch pried the girls away and stood with her arms crossed. "I will leave when I decide."

Hansel stepped toward the ladder, as if to leave, but then he stopped, closed his eyes, and rubbed the bridge of his nose with his fingers. "Lucie and Elsebeth," he said wearily, "will you play on the porch for a while, so I may speak to Marusch and Rudi? Thank you, girls." He smiled weakly after them as they skipped through the doorway to the outer room.

Rudi's nostrils flared. "You mean there's something else you haven't told us yet?"

Hansel shrugged. "I didn't think you needed to know. But now you do. Because Marusch needs to understand." He sat on the floor, and gestured for the others to do the same. After a deep breath, he began.

"Marusch, as I've told Rudi already, Gretel and I left here with our fortune after we escaped from the witch—to live happily ever after, some have said. But it was not easy to live happily, despite our new wealth, because our thoughts were never far from what happened to us in the witch's cottage. It haunted our dreams and waking hours alike. Gretel sailed away to escape her past, while I tried to understand it. I wanted to know: Who was Ulfrida? From where did such evil arise? Were there more like her?

"Kurahaven, my new city, was just the place to search for the answers. There are wonderous libraries there, and great scholars. Finally my search led me to a fellow named Umber, a historian who has compiled vast knowledge of all things strange and evil and monstrous. What I tell you now, I learned from him.

"Know this first, Marusch: North of here, on the far side of this great forest, this land ends in a peninsula. On the tip of that peninsula is Kurahaven, and the seas beyond are scattered with countless islands of all sizes. Some are large and teem with people. But farther from shore, the isles are more desolate and widespread. And one of those was infamous as the home of a great warlock—a man said to be centuries old, a mighty warlord of ancient times who discovered a way to preserve his life. His name was Vilikus.

"This island of his was strange and terrible. For countless years it was hidden under a thick fog that wept endless rain and never moved, no matter how hard the winds blew. Some who were brave enough to approach by boat came back with stories of hideous phantoms that rose out of the sea to frighten them away, phantoms so awful it could drive you mad to look at them. And others . . . well, others vanished into the mist and never came back at all.

"And then one day, nearly fifty years ago, the phantoms no longer appeared. Some brave men—or reckless fools, others would say—sailed into the mist and landed on the island to learn its secrets. The few who came back alive told of a great swamp in the center of that island. And in a tower in the middle of that swamp, they saw Vilikus himself: tall, gaunt, and ashy gray, like a skeleton wrapped in wet parchment. They said his eyes were as red as blood. And around him was a swarm of winking lights, also red, like tiny stars."

Rudi had kept one eye on Marusch as Hansel spoke. At the mention of the dark cloud, she drew her knees to her chest and hugged them.

"Vilikus had servants on his island," Hansel continued. "Creatures called murglins that lived in the swamp. They were the size of men, and they walked like men, but they looked more like the wriggling things you find under rocks in boggy places."

"Salamanders?" Rudi asked. When Hansel nodded, Rudi added, "Is that why Vilikus made it rain, then? For the swamp, and his murglins?"

"And to cloak his lair. That is what Umber believed. But it's those murglins that trouble me. I've never seen one, but I've heard about them. When you told me that strange creatures prowled these woods, I suspected the worst. But when that . . . *thing* almost found us in the cottage, and I heard the horrible sound it made, my fears were confirmed. It was a murglin, Rudi. I'm sure of it. And if the murglins are here, Vilikus himself may be here as well."

"He *is* here," Marusch said.

CHAPTER 7

Hansel stared grimly. "You think the warlock is here? Why so certain?"

Marusch pointed toward the curtained opening that led to the porch. "Go outside and climb higher. Tell me what you see."

Rudi looked at Hansel and nodded, and they went out onto the porch. The girls, who sat with their legs dangling over the side, smiled up at them.

Above, the ladder hugged the trunk of the great tree and disappeared into the branches above. "You go without me," Hansel said. "It takes all my daring just to make it this far up."

Rudi gripped the rungs and climbed, hand over hand and foot over foot. He rose past a heavy layer of branches that took him out of Hansel's sight, and passed a rope that was drawn taut between Marusch's tree and the next. *An escape route,* he assumed. He admired Marusch for taking every precaution.

The trunk narrowed as he ascended, and finally the ladder ended at a tiny round platform that Marusch had built around the tree, close to the top. There was no railing, so Rudi clung to the slender trunk and looked about him. And he saw it, many miles to the north.

Rudi had seen it before, of course, when he'd climbed the other tree to seek out Marusch's dwelling. But he thought then that he was looking at an ordinary pocket of fog. It was still there now, a great bank of gray that spun slowly and wept endless rain on the hidden place below.

He had been afraid it meant rain the first time he saw it. Now he knew it meant something far worse. His shoulders sagged as he beheld the warlock's mist.

Rudi let himself drop the last few feet onto the porch. When Hansel saw the look on his face, he closed his eyes and shook his head.

"Play here a little while longer," Hansel told the girls. Rudi followed him inside the house, and they sat again beside Marusch on the floor.

"I don't understand. *Why* is Vilikus here?" Rudi asked. "And what does he have to do with the witch you killed?"

Hansel rubbed a hand across his face, and continued. "The witch, the treasure—it's all part of the same tale. Let me finish. Vilikus stayed on his island for hundreds of years. But there were always those who waited for the chance to destroy him."

"Why? Why not just let him be?" Marusch asked with a hint of anger. "Perhaps that is all he wanted."

Hansel shook his head. "No, good lady. That is not all he wanted. Vilikus had an unspeakable appetite. Something he had in common with his daughters."

The word struck Rudi like an arrow. *Daughters.*

"Yes, daughters," Hansel added, noting Rudi's reaction. "Two of them, according to the lucky few who spied on Vilikus and escaped. One was Ulfrida, for sure. But her part in this tale comes later.

"Whenever a child vanished from one of the islands nearby, it was said that the murglins had come on their boats and taken him to their master. Finally, just ten years ago, a courageous army ventured at last to the isle of Vilikus. But when their boats arrived, they saw something utterly unexpected: The fog was gone, and the sun shone on the island for the first time in centuries. No murglins appeared to fight them off as they landed. The place seemed deserted. Umber himself was the first person to step inside the tower in the swamp."

Hansel paused to sip water. Rudi asked, "What did he find?"

"At first only some insignificant things: spare weapons for his murglins, dozens of empty barrels, and a room full of barren shelves that must have held hundreds of books. Umber found a single scrap of parchment on the floor, covered with words in a mysterious language.

"But Umber forgot about those things when he heard

a dreadful howl from the top of the tower. He and a few of the bravest fighters went warily up the stairs to find a locked door. A note on the door read: 'I leave you one treacherous daughter. Take your revenge on her. Vilikus.' They drew their swords and opened the door. And when they went inside, they found one of Vilikus's daughters in chains.

"From the way Umber described her, Gretel and I would have found her very familiar: a bent old crone with red eyes and snarls of white hair. She was raving mad, Umber said. It seemed she'd spent years locked in that tower. She screamed over and over again, '*She* betrayed him! It was *her*, not me!' Umber questioned her about Vilikus, but unfortunately, he was able to pry only a few answers from her. A group of angry soldiers stormed the tower, men with their own sad reasons to despise Vilikus and his daughters. Before Umber could stop them, they ended her miserable life. All he'd learned from her was two things: Vilikus had sailed away with his horde of murglins just a few nights before, hidden by the same mist that cloaked his island; and the warlock always had a few spies in his employ, people that lived among the regular folk and served as his eyes and ears. That is why the warlock left the island just before the attack. He had been forewarned.

"And that is the last anyone has heard of Vilikus. Rudi and Marusch, you may have already put the pieces of this puzzle together. But let me tell you what I think has happened—and when it happened. Nearly half a century ago, Ulfrida abandoned her father. This angered the warlock, probably because she took a fortune in gems and gold with her."

Rudi's hand had rested on the pack at his side. He folded his hands on his lap instead.

"So," Hansel continued, "he locked his other daughter in the tower, because she helped with the escape, or because he no longer trusted her. And I don't think he found out where Ulfrida had gone until a certain story reached his ears many years later: the story of her death, at the hands of two children."

"The tale of Hansel and Gretel," Rudi said.

"That's right. And when he was forced to flee his island, I suppose he thought he might as well inhabit the same forest that Ulfrida had chosen. A forest so deep and dark, it would be easy to hide there. And perhaps he could reclaim the treasure.

"So the vilest warlock of our times is here, Marusch. It's too dangerous to stay. One of his murglins knows that someone was poking about in the witch's cottage. And a white bird—another of his servants, I'm sure—saw Rudi and me in the forest. Vilikus will hunt for us. We can't stay another minute; we may have already waited too long. And you can't stay either. Come with us!"

"I'm not going anywhere," Marusch said.

"What do you mean? Haven't you been listening?" Rudi shouted at Marusch.

"Mind your tongue, boy. I am well hidden here. If the threat grows, I will move again, farther away. But this forest is my only home."

There was nothing more any of them could say. No arguments, warnings, or pleas could change her mind.

Finally Rudi stood with his feet on the ladder, the last to descend. In his pack was his entire share of the jewels, because Marusch still would accept none.

"The girls and I are leaving the village," he told her. "I don't think we'll ever see you again."

"I know. Say nothing of me to anyone."

He nodded and moved down the ladder.

"Wait," Marusch called. Rudi looked up at her face. It occurred to him that he no longer found it ugly.

"It made me glad," she said. "To have the girls here, I mean. And to meet you. I thank you for that. I hope you all live happily."

"I believe we will," Rudi said, smiling. "As happily as can be expected, anyway. Good-bye, Marusch. Be careful." He climbed partway down the tree, and glanced up to make sure she could not see him. He found where an enormous branch had broken away from the trunk many years before and left a deep hollow behind. Inside he placed a gold necklace with a fat diamond pendant and a pile of other gems for Marusch to find, when they were long gone and she could not refuse the gift.

CHAPTER 8

Uncle Hempel hunched over a wooden bowl at the kitchen table. When Rudi walked in, he lifted his head and smiled, and a mouthful of soup dribbled down his chin.

"Agnes!" he cried. "Rudi is back! But Rudi, where are the girls?"

"The girls are fine. Not that *she* cares," he said as his aunt turned around to scowl at him with her fists on her hips.

"Where have you been?" Aunt Agnes barked. "There's work to be done."

"Then you'd better get to it," Rudi replied, "because I've only come to say good-bye, for all of us."

Uncle Hempel's eyes grew moist. "You're leaving? But who will take care of you, Rudi?"

Rudi crossed his arms. "Don't worry about us. We'll be fine."

"Who put you up to this—that mapmaker?" Agnes said. Her jaw was clenched, and her right eye twitched.

Rudi looked at her and flashed a grin. "If you knew the whole story, and how happy we're going to be, I think your head would explode."

"Isn't that a thing," Uncle Hempel said, wiping the broth from his chin with his sleeve.

Rudi turned and walked away without looking back. Soon he caught up with Hansel and the girls, on the road to the village.

"Did you enjoy it as much as you expected?" Hansel asked.

"Oh, yes," Rudi lied. The truth was that even though he'd wanted this badly, he felt like crying. "Now let's get away from here."

"The faster the better," Hansel said. He took the girls by the hand to lead them.

The village was a few miles away, where the road that hugged the forest met a larger thoroughfare from the south, and enough travelers passed through to justify a lively trade. Hansel breathed a sigh of relief as they drew close, for the girls had bombarded him with questions about his adventure with Gretel. "Remember, children," he said, "not a word about the jewels. And don't call me Hansel. Call me Horst, until we're far away from here. We don't want to make anyone curious."

It was dark when they arrived. Rudi saw the silhouettes of familiar buildings against the starry sky, but also some unfamiliar shapes in the field between the town and the forest: tents and pavilions and tall wagons and other temporary structures.

"The harvest fair!" he exclaimed. "I'd forgotten about it."

"Oh, the fair!" cried Lucie. "Can we go in the morning?"

"That would be all right, wouldn't it?" Rudi asked Hansel.

"I suppose. Not for long though, children," Hansel said. "Tomorrow we'll leave on the first wagon I can find." The girls moaned their disappointment.

"It's all right," Rudi said, squeezing their hands. "There will be other, better fairs. Come now, we'll sleep in the inn tonight—you've never done that before!"

Rudi woke to the sound of knuckles rapping on the door of the room that he shared with the girls. There was a jingling sound as he sat up in the bed; he'd slept with the bag of jewels clutched to his chest.

He cracked the door open, and Hansel's face appeared in the slit. "I've found a driver who'll take us a good way down the road. To the next town, at least. We leave at noon."

Before Rudi could reply, Lucie sprang from the bed she shared with Elsebeth. "Then we have time to go to the fair!"

"Yes," Rudi laughed, "for a little while, anyway. Come on, *Horst*. I'm hungry, aren't you?"

They stepped outside into the golden sunlight and

squinted at a brightness they hadn't seen for days. Rudi thought the fair might be the only thing he would miss about Waldrand, and he reveled in its familiar sensations. There were jugglers and tumblers. Minstrels sang, children raced about and played foolish games, men cheered for archers, and townsfolk haggled over the price of goods. There were rabbits and birds in cages, and ducks, pigs, cows, and sheep in makeshift pens. He took a deep breath, and his nose was filled with the intoxicating smell of pies and meats roasting over open flames.

Rudi asked Hansel to buy the things he wanted for himself and the girls, so nobody would wonder where the poor boy that never had a pfennig to call his own had gotten his riches. "I'll pay you back, Hansel—I mean Horst," he said as they bought a pie. He glanced about to see if anyone noticed his mistake.

"My treat," Hansel said.

The girls rushed up and tugged at Rudi's arms. "Rudi, Rudi," Lucie cried, "come and see the puppet show with us!"

"Puppet show? Oh, that's what that is," Rudi said, looking at the tent that had been set up, apart from the others, close to the forest. Its canvas door had been tied shut earlier, but now it was pinned to one side. A performer was at the threshold, wearing a robe so long it brushed the ground and an enormous mask that looked like the head of an exotic, long-feathered bird. Over one hand the performer wore a puppet—a madly grinning, pop-eyed jester—and the other, gloved hand beckoned children to enter the tent.

"You go, Lucie and Elsebeth," Rudi said. "I just want to sit and eat."

He watched the girls run for the tent. He hadn't wanted to say it aloud, but he suddenly felt too old for puppet shows. Despite the fortune hidden in his pack, a melancholy hung over him, like the dark cloud over that shadowy place in the woods. A year ago, he'd have rushed to be in the front of the audience. But now . . . after what he'd seen and learned these past few days, it was as if a part of him had been left behind somewhere in that forest.

Lucie and Elsebeth ran past the silent puppeteer, giggling and holding hands. A few more children went in, and then the performer backed through the door and pulled the canvas across the opening behind him . . . *or her*, Rudi thought. It was impossible to tell, the way the entire figure was concealed by mask and robe and puppet and glove.

"What's the matter, Rudi?" Hansel asked.

Rudi realized he'd been staring at the door of the tent for nearly a minute. The canvas was being pulled taut, almost as if the puppeteer was sewing it shut from behind, from top to bottom. *With all the children inside.*

"I . . . ," he began, but words did not come to him. He walked toward the tent, awkwardly at first, because a creeping panic numbed his senses. The short distance seemed endless. Another young boy raced by him, late for the show, and pushed at the rectangle of canvas. It did not budge. He looked up curiously as Rudi arrived.

"It won't open?" Rudi asked, choking the words out of his constricted throat. He slid his fingers into the narrow gap at the edge of the canvas and tugged, but it held firm. Rudi put his ear to the cloth, but heard nothing. *No sound from a tent full of children?* he thought. His mouth had gone dry.

"Elsie! Lucie!" Rudi bellowed, but there was no answer. Some people nearby heard him and saw the fearful look on his face. They hurried over and asked what was happening.

"Something's wrong, we can't get in!" Rudi shouted.

A man next to him said "Here!" as he reached down to pull the side of the tent up from the ground. Something narrow and sharp pierced the fabric and plunged into the ground next to the man's foot, and he stumbled back in surprise. Rudi stared at the thin silver spearhead and dark shaft of polished wood, and cried out as he realized he'd seen one like it before. Then he was pushed aside by a man with a patch over one eye, who wielded an enormous knife.

"Fye!" the man cried, calling the name of a girl that Rudi knew from the village. "I'm coming, Fye!" He slashed once and then again, in two slanted strokes that met at the top. Only a few threads kept the triangular flap from falling open. The man raised the knife to strike again—but before he could, something inside the tent tore the canvas door away. The gathering crowd gasped, and in the full light of the sun Rudi saw the kind of creature he'd only glimpsed from his hiding place in the witch's oven. And he remembered Hansel's name for these things: *murglins*.

The murglin was nearly as tall as a man, with a serpentine body, short arms and legs, and a muscular tail. Its gray skin glistened with moisture. At the end of a long neck, its face widened like a newt's. The creature had huge eyes like spheres of black glass, set far apart. Its nose was just a pair of pinholes over a broad mouth that was now open, hissing at them, showing a deep throat lined with white ridges, each studded with tiny, pointed teeth.

People screamed. A woman next to Rudi seized her hair with both hands and pulled it. The man with the knife overcame his shock and stepped toward the murglin, holding the shaking blade before him. "Where's my girl?" he shouted, then leaped back as the murglin lashed out with its spear, inches from his chest. The creature hissed and stabbed at anything that drew close, until men came with bows and arrows, and then it disappeared inside the tent.

For an infinite moment the crowd was frozen by shock. Finally Rudi bolted forward and leaped through the gap. He hoped the murglin wasn't waiting inside to stab the first person to enter.

But nobody, human or otherwise, was in the tent. All he saw were rows of crude wooden benches and a deserted stage with a simple puppet theater. Toys and candy were scattered across the seats and ground.

"Where have they gone?" the man with the knife called out as he followed Rudi inside the tent. Others rushed in behind him and shouted the names of their children.

"Lena!"

"Hendrick!"

"Fye!"

Rudi ran to the stage. There was a large sheet of paper bearing a hand-written note pinned to the curtain of the puppet theater. But he ignored it—he'd never been taught to read, after all—and went to look behind the theater. In the wall of the tent, he found a long slice in the canvas, large enough to step through. The branches at the edge of the forest reached close enough to scratch the tent.

"They're gone!" he shouted to the townsfolk behind him. "Into the forest!"

"Hold on," a man said. Rudi recognized the fellow— he was Tobias, from the village. The note was in his hands. "Who is Hansel?"

"*What* did you say?" Rudi said. There were nearly twenty people inside the tent now, men and women, and he saw Hansel among them. When his name was spoken, Hansel pushed through the crowd and headed for the door.

"Listen, all of you! I'll read it," Tobias shouted, clutching the note. "It says 'Bring me Hansel, the slayer of my daughter, and your children will be returned. Go to the house of my daughter in the forest, and you will be shown the way.'" He turned the note around so the people could see. "It's signed 'Vilikus.'"

Rudi's legs felt weak. People shouted over one another, question after question, without waiting for answers: "Who's Hansel?" "Slayer of my daughter—what daughter?" "Is this about the witch?" "Who's this Vilikus?" "What house?" And then one voice pierced through the chaos with the answer to at least one of the questions, and bellowed the same thing over and over again: "*That's* Hansel! *That's* Hansel!"

Finally the crowd heard this and turned to see whose voice it was. There was the pie man, pointing grimly at Hansel. Rudi remembered that this fellow had been nearby when he let Hansel's name slip just a few minutes before.

"You're wasting time," Rudi screamed. "Forget the note—we have to find the children!" But he was ignored as shouts erupted and furious men grabbed Hansel before he could slip outside the tent.

Then the pie man pointed at Rudi as well. "And that one was with him—the woodcutter's boy!"

Just as it seemed things could not get grimmer, Aunt Agnes stepped into the tent. She learned soon enough what was happening, and smiled as she raised her voice to be heard. "Listen to me! Those two were in the forest these last few days—consorting with witches, so it seems! Check their packs and let's see what they've been up to."

Men shouted their agreement, and there was nothing Rudi or Hansel could do to keep the packs from being pulled off their shoulders. And soon, after their blankets and provisions had been ripped out and tossed aside, out came the bags of jewels. The men and women tore the sacks, and the gold and gems and even the girls' necklaces spilled to the ground. They were covered an instant later by a writhing mass of grasping, clutching people, and as word spread of the fortune, more bodies piled into the tent and joined the fray.

A few minutes ago there had been a happy scene in Waldrand, all song and dance and laughter, but that was forgotten now. Some people, mostly the ones without lost children, seized what they could and ran out of the tent, with their prizes hugged to their chest or thrust deep in their pockets for safekeeping.

"What's the matter with you?" Rudi shouted at the mob. "They're getting away with the children!"

"He's right," Tobias called out. "I'll go after them. Who'll come with me?"

"Me," Rudi said. But his aunt ran up and seized his arm.

"Just a minute," Agnes said. "Don't let Rudi or Hansel out of your sight! Can't you see? They brought this evil upon us! They caused this mess!"

Tobias eyed Rudi and Hansel warily. "Fine, then. You folks keep an eye on these two. Kurt, Oskar, Erwin, come with me!" Three men, all fathers of the stolen children, followed Tobias through the slit and into the forest. As an angry throng surrounded him, Rudi saw Agnes grin with a wicked glint in her eye.

CHAPTER 9

Rudi and Hansel sat side by side in the middle of the field. A group of men with clubs and knives stood by and narrowed their eyes whenever one of them so much as scratched his ear. Hansel watched mournfully as the wagon that was supposed to take them away creaked down the road with four empty seats.

Rudi felt as if his stomach had been stuffed with ice. He knew he should be in the forest, trying to track the murglins and bring Lucie and Elsebeth back. The fortune was gone. Their comfortable, happy future had vanished. But for the moment, he only wanted to see the girls' faces again, to take their hands and lead them to safety.

"Hansel," he whispered, "did Vilikus write that note?"

Hansel's head drooped so low that his chin rested on his chest. "Who else?"

"How did he know you were there?"

"The bird," Hansel said, covering his face with his hands. "The white bird."

Hours passed at an agonizing pace. Rudi's spirits sunk further when he saw a defeated-looking Tobias lead the other men out of the forest.

"We lost them," he told the others, with his shoulders slumped. "We tried, friends, we tried."

"Then give Hansel to this Vilikus!" shouted Agnes, who lurked nearby. To Rudi the sound of her voice was like the stab of a knife.

Tobias crossed his arms and stared at Hansel, who never raised his eyes. "We don't have much choice, do we?" Tobias said. "Tell me, stranger, are you really Hansel? The Hansel we've all heard of?"

"Yes, he is," Rudi said when Hansel did not respond. Hansel looked at him blankly. "Hansel, please, Lucie and Elsebeth have been taken. How else can we get them back? Talk to them!"

Hansel took a deep breath to calm himself. He struggled to his feet like an old man. "Yes. I am that Hansel. The one you've heard of. And the one that note asks for. I won't fight this; I will go and offer myself in exchange for your children." Rudi saw him clasp his hands together to stop their trembling.

"Don't trust him. He's already lied about his name," Agnes screeched. "Bind him up and put him on a leash—"

"Be quiet, woman!" Tobias snapped. "You're awfully interested in getting your girls back, for someone who just tried to abandon them in the forest!" Agnes reeled back as if she'd been struck, and her face turned a deep red as she glared at Tobias. "Oh, yes," Tobias said coldly, "don't think we haven't heard about you. You couldn't care less about the children." Agnes whipped around and pushed her way out of the crowd.

"I care about them," Rudi said.

Tobias peered sternly down at Rudi. He was a furniture maker who'd bought plenty of oak and beech and cherry wood from Uncle Hempel over the years. He'd always been a reasonable fellow, but now there was a stony look in his eye that Rudi had not seen before.

"My Lena was in that tent," Tobias said to Rudi, before he turned to Hansel. His words were civil, but the tone was severe. "Your offer is appreciated, Hansel. But forgive me and the others if we think it necessary to accompany you. I'm sure you'd do the same, if your child had been taken."

Tobias lifted his head toward the crowd. "Who else will come?" Several men shouted out at once, all fathers of the stolen children. There was Kurt the coppersmith, Oskar the wheelwright, Erwin the candle maker, and the farmers Nikolaus and Georg.

"I'm coming too," Rudi cried.

"I think we'd better leave you here, Rudi," Tobias said, looking sideways at Hansel. Rudi understood the problem: Tobias didn't want Hansel to have an ally with him.

"Suit yourself," Rudi said. "But you won't reach the house in the forest without me. No offense, Hansel, but if you lead the way, the only thing you'll find is that you're lost." Hansel smiled sadly; he couldn't argue the point.

Oskar stepped up to speak quietly to Tobias. "That boy knows the woods better than us. We could use him."

"Fine," Tobias said wearily. He didn't look pleased with the decision.

"I suppose I'll come along, if nobody objects," came a gruff voice from behind them all. Rudi didn't have to look to see who had spoken. It was Burck.

Hansel shot a questioning glance toward him, and Rudi realized he'd winced when he recognized the voice. He gave a subtle shake of his head to Hansel, as if to say, *Don't worry.* Burck might be a crude, combative, cold-blooded fellow, but maybe they'd need someone like him if they were going to meet Vilikus.

Burck wasn't tall, but he was wide and strong, his arms knotty with muscle. He had hawkish features, with a brow that hung like a ledge over dark, deep-set eyes that were always half closed. His dark hair had receded at the temples and left a dagger-shaped patch that pointed to his nose.

He was a good enough hunter to earn a living at it. Whenever word came of a mad wolf in the woods, or a savage boar, a tight-lipped smile would come to Burck's mouth and a fierce spark to his eyes. He would gather up his bow and his knife (a blade so long it could almost be called a sword) and lope off into the forest. Some time later—it might be a day, it might be a week—he would return with the slain beast draped across his shoulders. Burck was not a man you bantered with, or even spoke to without good cause, and his only friend in Waldrand was the butcher who paid him for the animals he'd killed.

Now the hunter strode up and looked around at the group. His gaze lingered on Hansel.

"So you're Hansel, eh?" he said. Hansel turned his eyes skyward, closed them, and nodded. "I heard what happened this morning," Burck said, gesturing toward the tent. "Too bad I wasn't here."

Some of the men in the crowd murmured and nodded, probably thinking, *Of course, Burck would have killed that creature in a trice.*

"Of course we're happy to have you, Burck," Tobias said. He eyed the hunter uneasily. "I'd have asked if you hadn't offered. You know these woods better than any of us. But let's be clear: We're not going in there to fight or hunt or argue. We'll trade this fellow Hansel for our children, and then get home as fast as we can."

"Fine with me," Burck nodded. The hunter was grinning, but Rudi didn't like the gleam in his eye. He didn't like it at all.

CHAPTER 10

Rudi waited for the rest of the party to catch up with him and Burck. It was an odd assortment of men that came together for this journey, like a sampler of all the shapes that men could take. There was Kurt, short and square with thick legs and arms, and a patch over his missing eye; Oskar, the gangliest man in the village, with a comically long neck; Erwin, so thick and hairy that if he stripped he'd be mistaken for a bear; big-bellied, red-faced Nikolaus; and Georg, who was almost as slight and short as Rudi.

And then there was Burck, who assumed authority as soon as they stepped into the trees, by virtue of his knowledge of the forest, and the simple fact that he could crush any of the others in a fight.

They'd gotten a late start, and it was dark before Rudi could get close to Marusch's dwelling. Rudi dug out his flint and steel to start a fire, but it wasn't needed. Kurt had brought a hot coal preserved in wet leaves to make that job easier. Rudi slipped the flint and steel into his pocket. He'd return them to his kit later on.

They sat around the fire, and the men spread their blankets on the ground, getting ready to sleep. Burck was the first to snore; he was no stranger to sleeping in the woods. The rest stared nervously into the surrounding trees, with the blacks of their eyes grown wide. Their heads snapped to look whenever an owl hooted or a bat fluttered overhead or some tiny creature skittered among the dead leaves, and their hands edged toward the bows or axes or cudgels they kept by their sides. But exhaustion from the day's long walk finally took its toll, and they began to nod off.

Hansel was still awake, sitting with his back against a tree. He stared at the fire. Tobias had threaded a chain around a thick arched root and secured the other end to an iron band that was clamped to Hansel's wrist. They took no risk that their bargaining chip would sneak away.

Rudi edged toward Hansel, sliding across the ground as quietly as he could. It was their first opportunity to talk, since Rudi was leading and Tobias kept Hansel in the middle of the pack, where he could be watched. "I'm really sorry," Rudi said. He didn't know how else to begin.

Hansel sniffed and looked up at the black canopy of leaves and the few stars that glittered through the gaps. "We almost made it, didn't we, Cousin? If the cart was ready a little sooner . . ."

Rudi's shoulders fell. "We shouldn't have left the inn."

"At least," Hansel said, "the whole village knows how awful your aunt Agnes is."

"Yes. I wonder how they found out about what she did."

Hansel managed a lopsided grin. "I might have let a word or two pass to the innkeeper."

Rudi tried to return the smile, but couldn't sustain it. "I have another problem now."

Hansel nodded. "You have to go near Marusch's tree before you can find your way to the witch's cottage."

"What'll I do? It's the only way I can get us there."

"It'll be all right, Rudi. Just circle around her place, as widely as you can. But watch out for Burck—he's a nasty fox, that one." Hansel looked around to make sure no one was watching, then leaned closer and lowered his voice. "You saw me try to run this morning. When I heard what the note said."

"Yes," Rudi said. He couldn't look Hansel in the eye.

"There was a reason, Rudi. And it wasn't because I wouldn't trade myself for those children. There's something else I haven't told you yet."

That burning anger hadn't left him, Rudi realized. It only simmered, dormant in his belly. Now it flared again, and his hands curled into fists. "You're *still* lying to me? After all this?"

"Not a lie—just something I haven't mentioned yet. I told you, there's a reason. A good one."

"Fine," said Rudi. He let a long breath whistle sharply out his nose. "Tell me, then."

But before Hansel could speak, Tobias sat up and glared at them. "Rudi! Come away from him. I won't have you two plotting. Don't make me chain up both of you!"

Rudi moved to the other side of the fire, next to Tobias. But his thoughts stayed with Hansel, and what he'd been about to reveal. *What a maddening fellow*, Rudi thought. After all they'd been through, he hardly understood the man. Sometimes Hansel was a whimpering coward. But other times he was brave, like when he first met Marusch. But it probably wasn't Hansel's fault, Rudi conceded. This world, he was learning, was a mad place, with a wonder for every danger and a heartbreak for every joy. Maybe living in it for so many years made you so crazy you didn't know how to behave from one minute to the next. Maybe that's what growing up was about. *But what do you know?* he asked himself as he drifted off to sleep. *You're just a kid.*

The night died, a new morning was born, and the group was on its way again.

Rudi tensed as they drew closer to Marusch's dwelling. Behind him, he heard Hansel telling the others stories of Vilikus. He spared no detail, offering gruesome stories that he hadn't even shared with Rudi before. The men were rattled. Georg swiveled his head left and right like a nervous bird, and Nikolaus wiped sweat from his forehead with his sleeve. Even Burck, who'd breathed down Rudi's neck the entire journey, fell a pace or two back so he could better hear what Hansel had to say.

Good idea, Hansel, Rudi thought. *Keep their thoughts occupied, while I steer us away from Marusch.*

Now he could see the top of Marusch's towering evergreen in the distance. He quickened his pace and veered left, beginning to circle around her dwelling so she would not be disturbed. But a minute later he realized that Hansel was no longer talking, and the tromp of feet behind him had ceased.

When he turned, a chill flashed along his spine. Burck hunkered low to the ground and held one finger up to silence the rest of them. He stared at the patch below him and tugged at an earlobe.

"What is it, Burck?" Kurt asked.

"Someone's been here. See?" Burck said. He pointed to where a little stand of ash saplings grew. Three of them had been neatly sliced at the bottom.

"A deer could have done that," said Nikolaus.

"A deer with a saw?" sneered Burck. Nikolaus's face went purple.

"Whoever it was tried not to leave too many signs," Burck said. "But there's a trail here." He pushed some leaves aside. "And a track."

"Is it one of those . . . *murg*-things?" Erwin's voice wavered.

"No," Burck said flatly. "It's a man. Or a boy—the feet aren't that big. Might even be a woman."

Rudi's mouth had gone dry. *No, no*, he pleaded silently. So much had been spoiled already—for him, for the girls, for Hansel. He couldn't bear seeing Marusch's life in ruins as well. "Are you coming or not?" he shouted to the men. His voice sounded like someone was squeezing his throat.

Burck looked up at Rudi from his squat, his mouth twitching on one side. Then he turned to the others. "Don't you think it's strange? Someone living so deep in these woods?"

"Let's go already," Rudi urged. He took a few more steps, praying that they'd follow.

"In a hurry, isn't he?" Burck said. It was an enraging habit that Rudi had noticed. The hunter never spoke directly to him. Instead he talked about him to the rest of the party, as if Rudi was a dog instead of a boy. Burck stood and brushed his hands on his chest. "Funny how the boy turned us to the side just then. After he led us straight as an arrow for so long. Think there's something he doesn't want us to see?" Burck flashed a smug grin, with his brutish lower jaw thrust forward. "Maybe we should follow this trail and see who it leads to." The way Burck stared at him, Rudi suddenly felt like one of the animals the cruel man hunted.

"What's the matter with all of you?" Hansel roared suddenly. "Your boys and girls are out there, and Burck wants to waste your time chasing some deer trail? Don't you know what this Vilikus does to children? Or have you forgotten what his daughter almost did to me?"

During the shocked pause that followed, all Rudi heard was his own nervous, labored breathing.

"He's right," said Nikolaus at last, biting his lip. "Let's just be on our way and follow the boy. We may be running out of time."

"What a sorry bunch of sheep you are," Burck growled. "Don't you see something's wrong?" He pointed a fat, hairy-knuckled finger at Hansel. "Why's he so eager all the sudden to be handed over to this warlock? I'm telling you, someone lives here. These two know who it is, but they don't want us to know. I don't like secrets, so I'm going to find out what the story is." He reached over his shoulder into the quiver that was slung on his back, pulled an arrow out, and notched it loosely on the string of his bow. "Wait for me here if you want, or go ahead and I'll catch up to you. You move like snails anyway." He broke into a trot, straight toward the tree where Marusch lived, perhaps a quarter mile away.

"I'm going with him," Rudi said, and he ran before anyone could object. Burck was ahead of him, running and tracking at the same time. He was like a hound on a scent, watching the ground for signs and the trees for danger.

The hunter stopped suddenly and squatted. He put one end of his bow to the ground and leaned on it for balance.

"What is it?" Rudi asked, coming up beside him.

Burck looked at him, quickly and dismissively, and stared at the ground again.

"Well?" Rudi pressed.

Burck straightened up and gave Rudi a longer look, pursing his lips. He seemed to be deciding if this boy was worthy of a response. "Your friend had some visitors."

Rudi gulped hard. He wondered if Burck had seen the tracks that he, Hansel, and the girls had left. "Some of those murglins, I'm guessing." Burck said.

"Murglins?" Rudi said hoarsely. Burck brushed past, ignoring him. Rudi followed, and gasped as they passed through a stand of trees and saw Marusch's dwelling in ruins.

The planks from her floor, the railing from her porch, the thatch of her roof, the pans and pots of her kitchen; all were scattered across the ground. To his left Rudi saw her oil lamp, crushed and bent. To his right was one of the glass jam jars that Hansel had brought. Burck kicked at the stick-and-twine ladder that lay in a twisted heap, and he peered into the branches overhead, with his bow and arrow at the ready.

Something metallic and yellow in a shrub nearby caught Rudi's eye. He reached down and plucked out the brass compass, the one he'd borrowed from Marusch. He wrapped his fingers around it and squeezed, eyes shut. *Don't be dead, Marusch,* he thought. *Tell me you saw them coming, and got away.* He remembered the rope that connected her tree to the one nearby, the one she might use to escape an attack, and he looked for it in the branches overhead.

"What kind of freak lives in a tree in the middle of the woods?" Burck muttered behind him.

"Why don't you shut up?" The words came out before Rudi could stop himself. A moment later his brain filled with hot sparks of light. He fell to his knees and toppled onto his side, dizzy with pain. Burck had struck him across the back of his head!

"Who do you think you are, talking to me that way?" the hunter said. Rudi could barely hear the words through the ringing in his ears. "It's you that needs to shut up, you little snot."

Rudi had to blink hard to clear his vision. He saw Burck staring down with an angry, satisfied smile on those lips. Now the hunter waited, probably hoping Rudi would lose his temper and say something rash. But Rudi just lay there with his breath hissing between his teeth.

Burck nudged Rudi's side with the tip of his boot. "Who was it, boy? Who lived in that tree?"

Rudi fingered the tender, angry swelling on the back of his skull. "Just someone who wanted to be left alone. She knew the forest—helped us find the witch's house. But it doesn't matter anymore. She's either dead or run away."

Burck snorted. "*She*, huh? Why'd she want to be left alone?"

"She looked . . . *different*. And you know how stupid people can be about things they don't understand."

Burck's fist tightened around his bow. His lip curled on one side as he tried to guess if he'd just been insulted. "Tell me something," he finally said. "Are there any more jewels left in that witch's house?"

Rudi shook his head. "Jewels? That's why you wanted to come along? You'll be disappointed."

Burck's expression darkened. He jabbed Rudi with the end of his bow. "Never mind. Get up. Time to get moving again."

CHAPTER 11

It was dark by the time they reached the stream that would lead them to the cottage. But the moon came up, nearly full, and Burck insisted that they keep traveling by its glow.

Finally they saw the little house and stable in the clearing, frosted by the moonlight. Only Burck seemed interested in entering the house. The others stayed outside, watching the yellow gleam of his lamp through the windows and listening to things clatter inside. *Looking for treasure*, Rudi thought.

"What do we do now?" Oskar asked. He eyed the cottage warily.

"Wait for someone to come and show us the way," Tobias said.

"Someone or some*thing*," Nikolaus muttered through his fingers.

"Perhaps in the morning," Tobias replied without confidence.

They made their camp in the clearing. Burck emerged from the cottage at last, in a sour mood. He glared angrily at Hansel.

It took some time, but Rudi finally slept. He dreamed of Kurahaven, Hansel's city by the sea. He and Lucie and Elsebeth ran toward it, but the faster they went the farther it shrank into the distance. Rudi slowly realized that the sensation of something pressing his shoulder was not part of his dream, but a hand that prodded him awake.

He opened his eyes and nearly shouted with relief when he saw Marusch kneeling beside him, her white face bathed in the orange glow of the fire. Before he could utter a sound, her finger moved from his shoulder to his lip, telling him to be still.

"What are you doing here?" she whispered.

"Oh, Marusch," he said, ignoring the question. "What happened?"

"Murglins. Too many to fight. I had to flee. I ask again: What are you doing?"

"It's my fault, Marusch. Mine and Hansel's. We did this to you. Now you have no home. . . ."

"I'm not a fool, Rudi. I kept another refuge for a time like this. Under the ground, instead of in a tree. Now answer my question."

Rudi ran a hand through his hair and across the still-painful lump at the base of his skull. "It's terrible, Marusch. Murglins stole children from the village—

they took Lucie and Elsebeth, too. There was a message from the warlock. He said he'll return the children if we bring Hansel to him."

Marusch rocked back at the mention of Lucie and Elsebeth's names. Her lips peeled back even farther, exposing all of her long, red-stained teeth, and her hands covered her eyes. Then a sound came from nearby—a high creak that could only come from a bowstring pulled taut. Marusch's arms dropped to her sides. She stared at the man who'd crept up unseen, and now stood ready to send an arrow into her heart.

"Don't move a hair on your face," Burck called out, loud enough to awaken the others.

There were shrieks and gasps from the men. Oskar shouted, "What is that thing? Kill it, Burck!"

"Not until we find out what it wants," Burck said. He edged closer, until the tip of his arrow was a yard away from Marusch's face.

"Don't you hurt her, Burck!" Rudi yelled.

The hunter ignored him. "Here to drink our blood, you devil? What are you—a vampire? Hobgoblin? Some abomination the warlock summoned?"

"Just a woman," Marusch said.

With stunning speed, Burck dropped his bow and drew his enormous knife. Marusch twitched like a cat, but could do nothing else, because the deadly blade was inches from her throat. Rudi put a hand to the ground and searched for something he could use to help: a stick to knock the knife away, a stone to throw, anything.

"Ugliest woman I ever saw," Burck said. The sinister smirk returned to his face. "Say, you must be the boy's friend. The tree dweller. Heavens, boy, how could you stand to look at her?"

"I've met ugly, Burck," Rudi said. "And she isn't it."

Burck sneered down at Marusch, and something at her neck drew his eye. The smile on his face faltered, then came back even wider. "Well, what's this?" He brought the tip of the blade to her neck and used it to lift the golden chain she was wearing, and out from her shirt came the fat diamond pendant. It sparkled brilliantly by the light of the fire. "A bit of the witch's loot?"

Marusch snarled, and her hand came up to strike his arm. She was fast, but Burck was quicker still. With the composure of a man who'd been in countless scraps, he drew the knife back and used his free hand to grab her by the wrist. He twisted her arm to spin her around, and pushed her to the ground. Marusch struggled, but she was hopelessly pinned as he pressed his knee against her back. Burck clamped the knife between his teeth, and with his free hand tried to draw the chain over the back of her head. Marusch dug her chin into the ground to keep the chain from slipping off.

The rest of the men, except for Hansel, who was chained to a tree, stood and gathered around. Oskar had both hands on top of his head, Kurt gnawed on one of his fingers, Georg leaned nervously from foot to foot, and Nikolaus clutched his shirt.

"Maybe you're being a little rough on her," Tobias said.

"Look at those teeth!" Burck snapped. "She sneaks up to drink our blood and you say I'm being rough?"

"Leave her alone," Rudi said, his voice so low and fierce he even surprised himself. He stepped toward Burck with his hands tightened into fists.

"*What's that?*" Oskar yelled. He pointed at the cottage.

Through the half-open door Rudi saw something indistinct glowing with dull silver light. It drifted across the threshold and into the open, coming toward them, just a ghostly blob with a vaguely human shape. For a moment it dimmed and nearly faded entirely, only to come back stronger and resolve into something from a fevered nightmare. Arms sprouted from its sides like serpents crawling out of their dens, a head appeared at the top, and a hole opened in the middle of its face to become a terrible fanged mouth. The men screamed and put their hands, fingers splayed, before their eyes, trying to ward the specter off but still watch it at the same time.

Rudi watched, horrified, as the apparition grew. It was ten, twelve, fifteen feet tall, and its arms reached for them with long fingers that ended in needle-sharp points.

"It's the warlock—the warlock is coming for us!" bleated Kurt. Then he bolted away. Oskar, Erwin, Nikolaus, and Georg followed. Tobias hesitated a moment longer, then raced after the rest. The men disappeared into the trees, some screaming as they ran, some hunching to avoid the long clutching hands.

Burck was there still, pinning Marusch to the ground. He was petrified with awe as the specter drifted toward him. The ghost's mouth spread wider and grinned fiercely. A vaporous tongue emerged, growing longer and longer as it slithered through the air toward him. A silvery curtain spilled from its arms and formed vast bat wings.

Rudi's instincts bellowed in his brain. *Run!* But there was Marusch, trapped under the hunter's knee. And there was Hansel, chained to a tree, rocking in place with his head bowed.

Rudi could hardly believe what he was doing as he ran toward Burck and the phantom. He gathered all the speed he could in a few short strides, hurled himself through the air, and drove his shoulder into Burck's side. Burck grunted and sprawled on the ground next to Marusch. But the blow had snapped him out of his stupor. He scrambled away from the specter on all fours, then frantically rose to his feet and ran after the others. A strangled whine came from his throat as he fled.

"Come on," Rudi shouted, tugging on Marusch's sleeve. She snatched up her bow, and they dashed to where Hansel sat. Hansel still had his head lowered and his eyes squeezed shut. He looked as if he was trying to imagine that none of this was happening. Rudi saw

Marusch turn to stand between them and the specter. She raised her bow and drew an arrow from her quiver.

But what can an arrow do against a phantom? Rudi thought. He turned his attention to Hansel's chain, hoping Tobias hadn't secured it properly. But of course, he had. Rudi bit his lip. How could he tell Hansel that there was no way to save him—that they would have to run without him?

Hansel opened his eyes and looked past Rudi. "It's all right," he said wearily, as if he guessed Rudi's thoughts.

"I'm sorry," Rudi cried. He got up to run.

"It's gone," Marusch's calm voice informed him, and Rudi turned. Just beyond Marusch, where he'd expected the phantom to be looming, he saw . . . *nothing.*

Rudi felt woozy. He plopped down heavily beside Hansel. "Where . . . where did it go?"

"It just dissolved," said Marusch. "Like smoke in the wind."

"Imagine that," Hansel said.

"You're lucky," Rudi said, handing the key to Hansel.

Tobias had left the key in his pack, which they found discarded by the fire. Hansel popped open the lock. He tossed the manacle away and rubbed his wrist with the other hand.

"Do you think they'll come back?" Rudi said.

Hansel rolled his eyes. "Maybe. But I never want to see that Burck again. He's too cruel, too clever."

"Cruel perhaps, but not so clever," Marusch said. "He did not know you were being followed."

Hansel grinned. "Not many people would know if you followed them, Marusch. You move like a spirit."

"That may be so. But I was not talking about myself."

"*What?*" Rudi said. He looked at the trees behind them with alarm. "You mean murglins?"

"Not murglins," Marusch said. "A man. Strong but clumsy; it is amazing you didn't hear him blundering along behind you. Bigger than Hansel, and blond like Rudi. He carries a great ax on his belt."

"*What?*" Rudi said, echoing himself, but louder. "You must be joking. Is he still there?" Marusch didn't answer. Rudi cupped his hands around his mouth and shouted: "Uncle Hempel! You might as well come out. I know you're there!"

A long moment passed. Then some low branches in the distance rustled and parted. Hempel emerged into the open and slunk toward them with his head down like a scolded dog.

CHAPTER 12

"No," Rudi said. "No, no, no, no, no."

"It's not up to you, Rudi," Hansel said. "I think he should come with us. We may need a strong back before this is over."

"You know what he tried to do to the girls!" Rudi bellowed, pointing at his uncle.

"You told me it was all your aunt's idea," Hansel said.

"It was," Hempel said meekly. "I know it was bad, Rudi. I can see that now. I should never have listened to Agnes. But you know how I get." He rapped his knuckles against his head. "I'm not like you, Rudi. I don't think right sometimes. But now I want to make it better between us. I want to help get the girls back. That's why I followed you. Tobias and the others wouldn't let me come when I asked, so I had to sneak after you."

Rudi turned his back. "I wish you'd just go home."

Hempel tucked his head low between his shoulders and looked at Hansel, silently pleading. Rudi felt a hand grasp his forearm. Marusch pulled him aside.

"Your anger colors your judgment," she said quietly. She looked at Hempel, appraising him, and her eyes went to the great wide-bladed ax that hung from his belt. Hempel turned away, red-faced. He'd been afraid to look at Marusch ever since he first saw her.

"Is he as strong as he looks?" Marusch whispered.

"He's all muscle, except for his brain," Rudi muttered. He crossed his arms. "Fine. You both want him to stay? I guess I'm outvoted. But I don't trust him."

A grin appeared on Hempel's face. "You can trust me, Rudi. You'll see." The smile vanished quickly. "But, Hansel, shouldn't we get out of here? What if that thing comes back?"

"It won't," Hansel said. He saw the questioning looks of the others and didn't wait for them to ask. "I know because of something I haven't told you until now." Rudi groaned and threw his arms to the sky. "I know, I know, Rudi," Hansel added. "But this is the last secret."

"There's always one more secret with you," Rudi snapped. "I don't believe you anymore."

"Did it ever occur to you that there are some things you're better off not knowing? I may have kept secrets, Rudi, but I did it for a reason. This is dangerous information. But I swear on my soul, I'm revealing it all to you now. I'll tell you why I really came back. And maybe you'll think better of me once I've said it. Sit down, all of you; this will take a minute.

"Remember when I told you about Umber and the army that went to the island of Vilikus? I told you that all they found there was the witch-daughter, the empty barrels, and a scrap of parchment in a language that could not be understood. There was more to it. You see, Umber realized that the parchment was written in the same language as a five-hundred-year-old book that he owned—a codex that was rumored to reveal secrets about Vilikus. He redoubled his efforts to decipher the codex, and finally, just last year, he was able to break the code."

Rudi's curiosity finally overcame his anger, and he listened carefully to Hansel's words, sensing their importance. Marusch sat cross-legged on the ground and listened, with her bow across her lap and an arrow at the ready. But this was all too complicated for Hempel; he spent the time stealing glances at Marusch.

"Some of what Umber learned from the codex is what I've already told you," Hansel continued. "But there were other things you should know. It said that Vilikus cannot be killed by the sword—the magic that has kept him alive for hundreds of years has also made him indestructible. It tells us about the murglins, the race of creatures he has bred over the centuries to serve him. And it tells us that water is this warlock's element—he has the power to manipulate it, which explains that perpetual cloud of rain.

"But more important, the codex revealed the secret of the terrible phantoms that guarded his island. They were *illusions*. Illusions that Vilikus created, with the help of a magical object.

"The object goes by many names: The *Simulapis*. The *Seonstan*. The Illusion Stone. The Eye of the Warlock. The scroll said that whoever possesses it can conjure any vision they desire, merely by focusing their thoughts on the stone." Hansel stared at Rudi and raised his eyebrows. "*Any* vision," he said again.

Thoughts connected in Rudi's mind; old stories and new experiences clicked together like the pieces of a wooden puzzle. "The Illusion Stone," he said as Hansel nodded. "Ulfrida must have taken it when she ran away from Vilikus! That's why the phantoms disappeared from the island fifty years ago. And Ulfrida had the Illusion Stone with her in the cottage, so when you and Gretel saw it . . ."

Hansel nodded faster. "We imagined we saw a house made of gingerbread and candy. But that was what the witch Ulfrida *wanted* us to see. It was an illusion designed to lure children into her clutches. It could have been anything, though. It could have been puppies and kittens."

"I like puppies," Hempel interjected. Marusch raised her eyebrows and gave him a look Rudi hadn't seen before—bemusement, he supposed.

"So do I, Hempel," Hansel said.

Rudi gaped at Hansel. "But now *you have the stone.*"

"Yes. And that's why I can assure you that the specter won't come back." Hansel smiled crookedly. "It's just something I saw in a nightmare once. I envisioned it, and you all saw it. Because of this." He reached down the collar of his shirt and drew out the crude chain until the ruddy, eye-shaped stone in its iron cage dangled below his fist. "The Simulapis. The Illusion Stone. This is what the warlock is after. He only wants me because he suspects I have it, or that I know where it is."

"So that's why you wanted first choice of the witch's treasure," Rudi said. "Why wasn't it lost with the rest of our jewels, back in Waldrand?"

"This was too precious—I sewed it into the lining of my shirt to hide it," Hansel said.

"It doesn't look precious," Hempel said, scratching the top of his head.

"No, it doesn't," Hansel agreed. He looked nervously at the trees around him and stuffed it back down his shirt. "But to Vilikus, there is nothing more valuable. When he possesses it, he can create such fearsome illusions that no man would have the courage to approach him. Or he can make a ship's captain see safe passage in a strait where deadly rocks will sink the vessel. That's how the Illusion Stone protects him. Without it, he is vulnerable. He fled his island and came all the way to this forest so that he might wield it once again."

"Wait," Rudi said. "If he can't be harmed by weapons, then how is he vulnerable?"

"If captured, he could be locked in a dungeon. Or sealed in a tomb," Hansel said. "And who knows what means he uses to preserve himself? Perhaps if those were taken away, his longevity would end."

Marusch finally spoke. "So Vilikus must never have the stone again."

"Exactly," Hansel said. "I came back here hoping that he hadn't discovered the hiding place yet. But now look where fate has brought me—almost into his clutches."

"So what do we do?" Rudi asked.

"Good question," Hansel replied. He turned his face toward the sky, which flushed pink toward the east; a new day was near. "The problem is that Vilikus believes I have the stone. One of his murglins saw where the treasure had been unearthed, and then that accursed white bird of his saw Rudi and me in the forest. So unless I bring the stone with me, I can't just surrender myself to him."

Rudi sat upright. "What do you mean, you can't? We have to get Lucie and Elsie back—and the others!"

Hansel pressed the heel of his hand against his temple. "Rudi, haven't you been listening? Don't you see what kind of monster we're dealing with? It's not me that Vilikus is after—it's the stone. And we can't give it to him."

"Yes we can, if that's the only way to save the girls!"

"Oh, look at the bird," Hempel interrupted. He

pointed at the crumbling roof of the house. The white bird was perched on the chimney, with its head turned sideways to behold them.

Go to the house of my daughter in the forest, and you will be shown the way. That's what the note from Vilikus had said. It didn't surprise Rudi that the white bird would be their guide, just as a white bird had led Hansel and Gretel into danger so many years before.

The bird stretched its wings wide, hopped off the chimney, and glided down. It landed on a stump just a stride away and opened its beak to caw. There was a blur of motion as Marusch sprang to her feet, pulled back on the string of her bow, and fired an arrow. It struck and the bird's caw became a piercing shriek. It fell off the stump, and as they stood and watched, its white feathers fell away to reveal a pale reptilian creature. It raised its head and hissed at them with its tongue rattling inside its mouth, until it lay still on the ground.

"Marusch, have you lost your mind?" Rudi's legs went soft beneath him. He dropped to his knees and clasped his hands atop his head.

Marusch ignored him. She walked over to examine the bird, and prodded it with the end of her bow. "Wicked servant to a wicked master."

Rudi's temper exploded again, and his voice came out loud and shrill. "We needed that bird to take us to Vilikus! How can we get the girls back now?"

"Calm yourself, boy," she said. "Would you really walk

in and surrender the precious object to the warlock? Did you hear what's at stake here? Or has the roar of your temper made you deaf?"

"You just doomed them, Marusch! The girls, and the rest of the children!"

"Now, Rudi," Hempel began, but Marusch raised a hand to silence him.

"Hear me out, all of you," Marusch said. "Hansel, you have told us about this Vilikus, and the depth of his evil. Tell me truthfully: Can he be trusted to keep his word? Do you believe the children will be spared if you sacrifice yourself?"

Hansel stood for a while, tugging at his nose. "No," he finally replied. "I don't believe that. I wish I did, but I don't. He won't let his captives go, to tell the world what they've seen. We'd be like flies trusting a spider. That's how wicked this warlock is."

Rudi's anger flashed like a bolt of lightning that needed a place to strike. "You're a fine one to speak of trust! You haven't been truthful from the beginning. Now you say there's no point to sacrificing yourself. How do we know you're not lying again, to save your skin?" Even as the words came out, Rudi was ashamed of himself for speaking them.

Hansel looked down at him with glossy, wounded eyes. "There's a difference between lying and holding back part of the truth, Rudi."

"Well, it feels the same to me."

"I had my reasons for not telling you everything. Do you think I liked deceiving you?"

"Enough, both of you!" Marusch said. But she was glaring at Rudi. "This is what I propose: We will go to Vilikus's lair. But we will not be led there like sheep to the butcher. Let us creep up unseen and learn what we can. Perhaps we can free the girls without sending Hansel to his doom."

For the first time since his name was found on the note from Vilikus, a new spark of hope kindled in Hansel's eyes. "It sounds like a wise course to me. Though I worry about bringing the stone so close to the very being that must not possess it."

Rudi pointed at the dead reptilian creature. "Hasn't anyone been listening? This . . . *thing* was supposed to guide us to Vilikus. But Marusch killed it!"

"We need no guide," Marusch said.

"What? You know the way?" asked Hansel.

"Anyone can find it. Look up."

Rudi, Hansel, and Hempel craned their necks, wondering what she meant. "Keep looking," she said. In the brightening sky that was visible above the clearing, Rudi saw scraps of low-hanging clouds sweeping to the north, toward the heart of the green forest. They moved swiftly; too swift, in fact, for such a windless day, and Rudi realized it was the warlock's magic that drew them. A new cloud, the same one he'd glimpsed from the tree-tops, hovered over the dark heart of the forest, just as one had once brought the rain to the warlock's island in the sea. Rudi watched another bit of cloud fly by and chided himself. *It's so obvious,* he thought. *You'd have to be an idiot not to notice.*

"I don't see anything," Hempel said, squinting up.

Marusch went into the trees at the edge of the clearing and returned with a pack of her belongings. She fished out the blue glass to shield her eyes from the rising sun. "This way," she said.

Hansel touched Rudi's shoulder. "Rudi, before we go on, I want to tell you something."

"What?" Rudi muttered. He shrugged the hand off.

"I'm worried about you."

"Don't be," Rudi snapped.

"There. That's exactly what I want to talk about. You're far too angry, Rudi. Don't look at me that way— you're proving my point, don't you see? Listen, I know you have your reasons. You've been wronged, you've been lied to, you've been beaten down. But let me tell you something about anger, something I know from experience. It's like a fire, Rudi. Right now it can be useful to you, because it focuses you, and makes you stronger and braver than you might otherwise be. But it's only useful if you have it contained. A fire in a stove is a good thing, Rudi. It will warm you and feed you. But if the fire gets too hot, if you lose control—poof, there goes the whole house. The house of Rudi. Do you understand me?"

Rudi looked past Hansel's shoulder, with his eyes focused on nothing. He was angry, all right—furious that Hansel would worry about anything but getting the girls back alive. "Are you done lecturing me?"

Hansel stared at him grimly. "Sure, Rudi. I'm done."

They followed Marusch out of the clearing and left the rotting cottage behind.

I never want to set foot in a forest again, Rudi thought as they walked on and on through the long day, sharing what provisions they had. Overhead more and more flecks and wisps of fog appeared and converged on some central point still miles ahead. The deeper into the woods the group plunged, the thicker the air seemed.

"Rest, please!" Hansel groaned at last. He let his pack drop to the ground and lay on his back with his arms spread wide, too tired even to drink water from the skin that the others passed around.

"How far have we come, do you think?" Rudi asked.

"Twenty miles, perhaps," Marusch said. "Maybe more."

"I think we're getting close," Rudi said.

Hempel handed Marusch the skin of water and smiled broadly as she thanked him. It occurred to Rudi that something about Marusch had changed since he'd first met her. "Marusch, you sound different," he said.

Marusch nodded. "My voice was out of practice. For years I hardly spoke at all, with nobody around to listen. I was afraid I sounded like a madwoman, talking to myself, so I stopped. When I met the girls, I worried that I'd forgotten how to speak at all. I sounded horrible—I must have frightened them."

"Of course you didn't," Hansel said, propping himself up on his elbows. "Those girls loved you."

Rudi's shoulders twitched and he glared at Hansel. "They *love* her, Hansel. Not loved. *Love*. Do you hear me?"

Hansel lay back on the ground again. "Of course, Rudi. That's what I meant."

CHAPTER 13

An hour later they stood and looked at the fog that blotted out the sky. Behind them more shreds of cloud drifted close and were swept into the pale mass. The fog was thickest overhead, where it swallowed the tops of the tallest trees.

Up to that point the sun had still peeked down now and then through the misty, spiraling arms. But the next few steps would take them into sunless gloom.

"This is it," Hansel said. "His domain." It was a warm day, but Rudi shivered nonetheless. Marusch took the tinted glass from her eyes and stuffed it in her pack.

"I don't like the way it feels here," Hempel said. Rudi had to agree. It was more than just the murky light. There was an unmistakable aura of foreboding, something he could feel in his bones. None of them moved.

Look at us, frozen like rabbits, Rudi thought. He closed his eyes and pictured Lucie and Elsebeth. What was it he'd promised them not so long ago? *I will go anywhere to bring you back. I will fight anyone who means to harm you.* He stepped forward, into the shadow. "Come on, let's go find them," he said. And the rest followed.

The landscape began to change. Everything shone dully, and the trees ahead faded into ever more ghostly shades of gray. Rudi saw the reason: a fine mist suspended in the air. As they walked on, the mist began to move. He stopped and held his hand out in front of him. Yes, he could see that the infinitesimal drops of water were slowly falling. He watched them collect along the thin hairs on the back of his hand.

"Rain," he told the others.

Hansel nodded. "Just like his island. Vilikus always brings the rain," he said.

"But why?" Hempel asked. "Why would he want it to rain all day?"

"No one is sure, Hempel. Perhaps he needs the mist to cloak his lair, or to breed his murglins. Or perhaps there is another reason that we don't know."

"It's not good for the trees," Hempel said. "Too wet, and no sun."

His uncle was right, Rudi could see; the trees grew sicker the farther they walked. Rotted leaves and dead branches cluttered the ground, and many trees had fallen. White ridges of fungus and oozing yellow slime clung to bark that was blackened by the damp. Only the feathery ferns and slick mushrooms truly flourished.

Then there was the odor. Rudi wrinkled his nose. It

reminded him of the smell water had when it sat in a rain barrel for too long, and tiny, nearly invisible things wriggled and swam inside it; it smelled like when he pulled a rock out of the muck to see what lived underneath. It was the scent of slugs and frogs, centipedes and snails.

Farther under the cloud, they heard the spatter and pop of falling drops as the mist collected on leaves and branches and dripped onto the ground below. They walked as quietly as they could. The earth squished under every step.

Suddenly Hempel caught his foot on a branch and stumbled. He put his hands on the trunk of a dead tree to steady himself. But the tree was so thoroughly rotted that it began to list to one side—slowly, so Rudi thought it might not topple at all. But then it sagged beyond salvation. Its trunk wrenched apart with a groan, and the tree slammed into the ground with a great damp *thump* that was swallowed by the mist. Beetles scrambled and termites writhed in the ragged yellow pulp where the stump had broken. Hempel watched all of this with his hand clapped over his mouth.

"What's the matter with you!" Rudi hissed. "Are you trying to get us caught?"

"Hush, boy," Marusch said. They peered into the trees around them, waiting to see if the sound had betrayed them.

After some minutes passed, Marusch took a deep

breath. "All the trees here are dying; one must fall every day. Even if the warlock's servants were close enough to hear, they might not think anything of it." She put a hand on Hempel's shoulder and cast a fierce glance at Rudi. "But an angry shout might bring them running."

Rudi turned away as his face warmed. *There goes your temper again*, he scolded himself. "Let's just keep going," he muttered, and he led the way without looking back.

From somewhere ahead there came the splash and trickle of water in motion. It was the kind of sound Rudi usually loved to hear. But not here, where everything seemed steeped in evil.

"Quietly now," Marusch said. She stepped in front of Rudi to lead once more.

They crept forward and darted from tree to tree. Through the gloom they perceived a wide, dark smudge that stretched out of sight to the right and left. As they moved closer, they saw a kind of wall, built of logs, twigs, mud and stones. It was as high as the side of a barn. Its shape was irregular at the top, with countless jagged sticks pointing in every direction. The wall curved subtly away from them, as if it formed a giant circle that hid whatever lay on the other side.

"It's a dam," Hansel said as the same thought occurred to Rudi. Water trickled over the lowest points along its top. There were small leaks in many places, and Rudi noticed one sizable hole where water gushed out in a jet. Marusch tapped Rudi on the shoulder and pointed. Just

Catanese

visible in the distance through the fine mist, a murglin walked on the wall. The four of them hid behind a huge ailing tree—the last one standing close to the dam—and peered at the approaching creature.

This murglin was different from the others they had encountered. *It's no taller than I am*, Rudi thought, but it certainly looked stronger; its legs and arms were thick with muscle. Across its shoulders it balanced a wooden pole, with twin buckets dangling from each end. As it came closer, Rudi and the others shrunk back behind the wide trunk, out of sight.

Still an arrow's flight away, the murglin halted above a small leak in the wall. It grunted as it shrugged the pole and buckets off its shoulders and rested them on the dam. Then it reached into a bucket with both hands, drew out a soggy mass of black muck, and disappeared over the other side. A few seconds later, the leak stopped.

"Making repairs," Hansel said. They watched as the dripping murglin slithered up again. It wiped mud from its glossy black eyes, shouldered the buckets once more, and continued its patrol.

Good luck fixing the big one, Rudi thought. Until that moment the curve of the wall hid the gushing hole from the murglin's sight. When the murglin saw the leak, its mouth opened wide in an exaggerated expression of panic that nearly made Rudi laugh. The murglin turned toward whatever lay in the distance on the other side of the dam, tilted its head back, and unleashed a long, strange, gurgling howl.

Rudi and the others stayed hidden and waited to see what the murglin's cry had summoned. At last the narrow prow of a small boat appeared at the top of the dam, and six more murglins hopped onto the wall carrying more buckets. They dove again and again behind the dam, bringing masses of the muck down with them. The gushing leak slowed to a dribble and then ceased altogether.

"They don't like leaks very much," Hempel observed sagely.

Soon the boat and its crew were gone, and the first murglin wandered out of sight. "Let's go," Marusch said.

"Where?" said Hempel.

"We'll climb the dam and see what lies beyond."

Hansel cleared his throat. "Are you sure that's wise?"

"Stay here if you're too scared," Rudi said over his shoulder.

"It's not . . . I'm not . . ." Hansel shook his head and followed the others as they picked their way up the face of the dam, using the jutting sticks and rocks for handholds and footholds. Marusch was the fastest climber, and she stopped with just her head poking above the top. Hempel came next, and gasped when he looked. Rudi joined them a moment later, and finally Hansel. No one said a word as they beheld at last the great lair that Vilikus had created in the heart of the dark forest.

It was a vast lake, as flat and gray as slate. Overhead the mist was like a frothing brew stirred from above, with a white eye at its swirling center.

The dam did not encircle the entire body of water. It did not have to, for the land was higher on the other sides. Vilikus had corralled the waters with this crescent-shaped wall; rocky ledges and mossy hills did the rest for him.

This had been a valley once, filled with hundreds of trees. But when the water filled the valley, the trees drowned and collapsed, leaving only jagged stumps that stuck out of the water like blackened fangs.

Through the mist Rudi saw a cluster of islands in the center of this dismal lake. On the largest was a tall, round tower, built from crude slabs of dark rock. Some of the smaller islands around it were natural formations, where the land heaved up or great boulders lay. Low stone structures were built on these, and they were linked to the tower island by flat bridges. The smallest and most numerous islands were different: tiny, dome-shaped and built of the same stuff as the dam. *Homes of the murglins*, Rudi guessed.

The murglins' boat moved slowly across the lake. It was long, flat, and narrow, with low sides. At the stern two murglins propelled it, not with oars, but with long poles that could reach the bottom.

"Where do you think the children are?" Rudi said.

"There," Marusch answered, pointing. "The building

without windows. On the island nearest the tower."

That has to be it, Rudi reasoned. He stared at the low stone structure. It was hard to tell from this distance, but he even thought he could see a murglin at the building's door—a guard? His heartbeat quickened as he looked at the chain of bridges that connected that islet to the others. The chain ended not too far from the shore on their right. That would be the easiest path. *We can do this,* he thought.

"Something's in the water," Hempel said. Rudi followed his gaze, and saw to their left a disturbance in the lake. It was a moving mound of water that left a wide, rippling wake as something enormous swam just beneath the surface. Rudi ducked as low as he could while still peering over the edge, and he sensed the others doing the same.

A humped, ridged back broke the water's surface as the creature neared them, and they saw the same kind of mottled gray hide that they'd seen on the murglins. But whatever this was, it was far bigger.

"The size of that thing!" Hansel said.

As it drew close, Rudi saw dozens of strange little shapes clinging to the creature's back, each no more than a foot long. At first he thought they were eels, but as the beast swam closer, more details came into view: tiny arms and legs that clung to the gray skin, and bulbous heads with dark beads for eyes. *Eyes!*

"Get down!" Rudi whispered, and they all cowered behind the dam. They heard the rush of water go by, and a moment later the wake of the beast crested over the edge and doused them, one after the other. Rudi lost his grip and tumbled to the ground.

Hempel was beside him a moment later, and he lifted Rudi to his feet with a hand under each arm. "Are you all right, Nephew?"

"There's nothing wrong with me," Rudi said, twisting out of his uncle's grip. He shook his wet hands and wiped them on his shirt. "Hansel, what was that thing? Did you hear anything about a giant murglin from that Umber of yours?"

Hansel shook his head. "No. It seems like there are different kinds though, doesn't it? The ones that took the children were tall and thin. But the ones that work on the dam are short and thick. Maybe that beast was just another kind."

"Don't you see? It was the mother of them all," Marusch said, "with her brood on her back. But let us talk about what we do next—how to free the children."

"We can do it!" Rudi exclaimed. "We can get to that island easily enough. Did you see the way, Marusch?"

She nodded. "Yes. It will be dark soon, and that is when we will go. We will enter by the eastern shore, swim or wade to the first island, and then stay under the bridges, where we won't be seen."

"But that—that *thing* is in the water," Hansel said.

"Don't worry, Hansel," Hempel said, clapping him on the shoulder. "It must sleep sometime."

* * *

They moved back under the cover of the trees and then circled right, closer to the eastern shore. The land here sloped up toward a number of small stony hills.

"The warlock's rain filled this lake?" Hempel asked.

"Not only the rain," Marusch said. She pointed ahead. A stream surged down the slope and ended in a waterfall, spilling over a short cliff and splashing into the lake. It looked to Rudi as if the stream found its way out again through a notch in the ledge on the opposite shore.

They hid behind boulders and ferns and dead shrubs. As the light dimmed, they waited and watched. Rudi saw murglins ply the waters and move from island to island along the bridges. He eyed the stone tower, but never saw the warlock. But most of all, he stared at the low stone building for signs of the children.

"They're in there," Rudi muttered, trying to convince himself. He wished one of the kids would cry out so he could be sure.

"What about that murglin guarding the door?" Hansel said.

"If it is still there, we may have to do something about it," Marusch said. She ran a finger along the string of her bow.

"But, Marusch, we have a better weapon than your bow," Rudi said.

Marusch raised an eyebrow. Rudi pointed at Hansel's chest, where the Illusion Stone hung, hidden behind his shirt. "You can help us, Hansel. If there's trouble, use it."

Hansel raised his eyes to the dimming sky, and his shoulders sagged. "I didn't want Vilikus to get it, and here I am at his doorstep. I don't want him to know it's here, and now you want me to use it and remove all doubt? But fine, fine," he said, seeing Rudi about to protest. "I'll use it if we really have to. Oh, why did I ever come back? Gretel knew what she was doing. I should have sailed away with her."

The night came quickly after that, as if a curtain had been drawn behind the swirling cloud. Rudi expected to see the lights of torches or candles appear, but there were none. Only darkness.

"Come on," Marusch said, and she waded into the lake, holding her bow over her head with two hands. Soon the water rose as high as her chest.

"How deep is it?" Hansel asked. He eyed the water with an uneasy expression.

"Oh, just get in," Rudi said. "You're already soaked from the rain." He followed Marusch into the murky water. Hempel followed, and Hansel finally groaned and came after them. They moved out in a line, keeping the ragged stumps between them and the stone tower whenever they could.

Rudi's lip curled in disgust when his boot sank deep into the mire. Down there, everything that once grew now rotted under the still waters. Every now and then his steps tangled on the branch of some fallen tree, with its bark gone soft and its fine twigs gone rubbery. They waded through a place where a thin green slime sprawled over the surface. The water had an ill smell. He would never have dreamed of drinking it. *At least we don't have to swim*, he thought; that was a skill he'd never mastered. The lake here was shallower than where they'd seen the beast in the water, and it never came as high as his chin.

They reached the nearest island, and slipped underneath the first of the bridges. Marusch signaled for them to stop, and she peered up to make sure no murglins were about. As Rudi waited, his foot struck a strange object at the bottom. It was hard like a stone but lighter, maybe even hollow. He kicked at it, probing, and strangely, the toe of his boot slipped into a deep hole in the thing, so that he was able to bring it to the surface by lifting his foot.

"What *is* that?" Hempel whispered.

Rudi didn't have to answer, because they could all see that his toe was stuck in the eyehole of a skull. It wasn't a large skull. Rudi figured it was smaller than the one his own face masked. The lower jaw was gone, but tiny upper teeth were still in place. Something black and wormy wriggled out of the other eyehole, and Rudi kicked the skull off his foot in disgust. It sank and disappeared, tumbling, in the murky water.

"That was there for some time," Marusch said to Rudi. "It wasn't . . ."

"I know," Rudi replied before she could finish. He closed his eyes. *How many?* he wondered. *How many more are down there, just tossed into the swamp?* He opened his eyes again and looked back at the others. "We have to end this. We'll get the children out, but then we have to end this."

Hempel nodded vigorously, Hansel looked away, and Marusch only stared. "Another day, Rudi," she said. "After the children are safe. You will tell the people, and come back with a thousand men, and that will be the end."

They went on, creeping under the bridges and circling around the islands. Rudi saw that he'd been right about the little domed isles: A boat filled with a trio of murglins pulled up to one, and the creatures crawled through a hole into the hut of sticks and mud.

It was quiet except for the hiss of the tiny drops of mist hitting the still surface of the lake, and the distant splash of the waterfall. Strangely enough, it seemed to grow brighter instead of darker. Rudi figured the moon must have risen and infused the cloud with light from above. Near the eye of the cloud, where the mist was thin, the glow was cold and silvery.

They waded past the tower, so close that it eclipsed nearly everything else from view. It was even bigger than Rudi had expected, dominating the rocky island it sat on, with only a narrow band of stony land around it. Rudi looked up. He wondered if he'd catch a glimpse of the warlock in the narrow, barred windows. What was it Hansel had said? *"Tall, gaunt, and ashy gray, like a skeleton wrapped in wet parchment. . . . his eyes were as red as blood. And around him was a swarm of winking lights, also red, like tiny stars."* But he saw no crimson lights or skeletal shape in those windows, only black holes that stared down at him like eyes.

The isle with the prison—at least Rudi *hoped* it was a prison—was next. It was connected to the tower island by a long bridge that also served as a dock for three of the flat boats. The single murglin still guarded the prison door. It rested on a stump and leaned on one of those long, thin spears. Before they drew any closer, where the guard might hear them, Marusch waved them to her. They huddled together, out of sight between two of the boats. Their four heads bobbed inches apart.

"Has anyone seen that beast in the water?" Hansel said through chattering teeth.

"Never mind that," Marusch said. "We can open the door easily enough. It is not locked, only barred from the outside. But something must be done about the guard," she said. "What shall it be—the arrow or the stone?"

"The arrow," Hansel said. "I could conjure something with the Illusion Stone, but the murglin will call for help, won't it? We can't draw attention. It's better to silence the creature."

Marusch frowned. "I suppose it must be done. Though I feel like a murderess."

Then Rudi heard a sound that filled his soul with hope. Somewhere in that low stone building, a child began to cry. Not Lucie or Elsebeth, Rudi was sure; it sounded like a young boy.

"It's them! The children are in there!" he said nearly too loud.

The murglin rose from its stump and put its face to a small square hole in the wooden door. It hissed and the cries inside faded to a miserable whimper.

"Never mind what I said," Marusch said angrily. "I will pierce that foul thing's heart. I must tell you, though: I worry about my aim. My bow is soaked and my hands are numb."

"Let me do this," Hempel said. Beside him, his ax rose from the water. "I'll creep up behind it and knock it silly. With the blunt side, of course. If something goes wrong, there's always your arrow."

Marusch nodded. "But first, let us get as close as we can." She led them under the bridge. They waded to the edge of the prison island and hid behind a wide stand of grass, while Hempel went around the shore, half swimming and half crawling in the shallows. Once out of the guard's sight, he crept onto the land.

"Hope he does something right for a change," Rudi whispered. He felt a cold flutter in his stomach as he watched his uncle's silhouette vanish behind the building.

"You're too hard on him, Rudi," Marusch said. "He only wants to help."

It seemed as if years passed while they waited for Hempel to appear around the far side of the building. Marusch flexed her fingers to warm and loosen them, and slowly drew a dripping arrow from her quiver and notched it on the string of her bow. Hansel had his eyes half closed and his hand at his neck, clutching the crude chain that held the eye-shaped stone.

Finally Hempel poked his head around the corner. The murglin was just a few steps away. There was a bucket at its side. It raised its thin spear above the bucket, stabbed down, and drew it out again with a wriggling eel skewered at the tip.

Hempel slunk out from behind the building. He kept his left hand on the stone wall and held his great ax in the other hand, shifting his weight slowly from step to step with his heels never touching the ground. The murglin brought the tip of the spear to its mouth and chewed at the living eel. Hempel raised the ax.

It seemed as if it would proceed perfectly. But perhaps the murglin had sharp ears that caught the sound of Hempel's breath, or a keen nose that smelled him approaching. Whatever the reason, the murglin suddenly leaped off its stump and swung the spear toward Hempel, with half the eel still dangling from the narrow point. And worse still, the murglin opened its wide mouth and screamed. A chilling squeal echoed back from the high land on the sides of the lake.

Marusch stood, water streaming off her shoulders, and aimed her bow. The murglin thrust the spear at Hempel, but the powerful woodsman reached out with his left hand, seized the shaft, and pulled both spear and murglin toward him. The ax came down at the same time. The creature slumped to the ground, as limp as rope.

There were sounds now from around the lake. Murglins called out to one another from the islands and the dam. Rudi heard the splash of boats in the water and the slap of feet on the bridges, far away but getting closer.

"Come on," Marusch said, but Rudi had already scrambled onto the shore and raced for the prison door.

Hempel knelt over the murglin, making sure it was unconscious. "I'm sorry, Rudi. I tried to be quiet!"

"Just open the door, Uncle—hurry!" Rudi said.

Hempel lifted the heavy wooden beam that barred the door and threw it to the ground. Even before Rudi pulled the door open, he heard the high, hopeful voices of children inside: "What's happening? Is someone there?"

He stepped into the dark prison. "Hush, children, hush! You have to stay quiet! Are all of you here? Are Lucie and Elsebeth here?" Two little figures ran up and seized him around the waist.

"Rudi, Rudi! I knew you'd come for us!" Elsebeth said into his shirt.

"I knew it too! I told everyone you would!" Lucie cried.

Rudi kneeled and hugged them. "But the rest of the children—are you all together? The warlock didn't . . ."

"We're all here," another child said, grasping Rudi's sleeve.

"Then come with me as quietly as you can!"

CHAPTER 14

Rudi came out of the prison holding Lucie and Elsebeth by the hand. The rest of the children trailed behind in a line, clutching one another. In the glow of the moonlit cloud, Rudi counted the young ones. "Six, seven, eight—yes, that's everyone!" He recognized most of them from the village, and knew some by name: Lena the daughter of Tobias, Hendrik the son of Nikolaus, and Fye the daughter of Kurt.

"Trouble," Marusch said. In the dim light Rudi saw dozens of murglins tromping toward them on the chain of bridges that linked this island to dozens of others.

"Hansel?" Rudi called. But Hansel already held the Illusion Stone. His eyes were fixed on the crude gem, as if it was a knot he had to unravel.

The horde of murglins raced past the tower and onto the long bridge that connected to the prison isle. Rudi's head swiveled left and right, searching for some other way to escape. But what he saw confirmed what he already knew: the prison island was the end of the chain, a dead end with no more bridges leading elsewhere. They were trapped, and the warlock's creatures would be upon them in seconds. "Hansel!" Rudi shouted again, his voice rising in pitch.

Vapor appeared in the air before the bridge. The children gasped as it took on shape and dimension, as if it was milk pouring into an invisible mold. The vapor became a knight, clad from head to toe in silver armor that gleamed with spectral light. He was double the height of an ordinary man, with a broadsword nearly as long.

"Isn't that a thing!" Hempel shouted.

The knight came to life. He walked to the bridge, covering yards with every stride, and swung the enormous sword in great, deadly arcs before him. The murglins had nearly reached the island, but yelped and turned when they saw the mighty apparition.

Rudi was so transfixed by the vision that it startled him when Marusch's voice rang out loud behind him. "A change of plans—to the boats!" She was right, Rudi realized. A boat was their only chance now. They couldn't wade through the lake or cross the bridges to get past the murglins. And besides, even if the knight could clear the way, their flight would still take them past the tower, where Vilikus surely lurked—and was probably now rousing himself from slumber.

Marusch led them to the dock halfway across the

bridge. The knight strode before them and swept his sword back and forth, driving back the horde. The squeals and gurgles of the creatures littered the air.

"This one," Marusch said, pointing to the longest of the boats, with room enough for all of them. She untied the mooring rope and tossed it into the craft. "Hansel and Rudi in front, little ones in the middle, Hempel with me!"

Rudi climbed in beside Hansel, and Hempel shoved them away from the dock. The long poles that propelled the craft were stowed along the side. Rudi picked one up, plunged it into the water, and helped push them away. He heard splashing behind him and saw some of the murglins leap in and swim after them. Their slender bodies curled through the water like serpents.

"Marusch," Rudi called back, "the stream on the western shore!"

"Yes! That's the way!"

They poled furiously, and the boat picked up speed. Hempel was so powerful that they leaped ahead with his every thrust. Rudi put every muscle in his back and arms and legs into the effort. He looked back at the murglins, and was relieved to see them falling behind. *Thank heavens for that.* He glanced at the tower, but there was still no sign of the dreaded warlock. *Is he sleeping? Is he even here?*

Rudi thought the children would whimper or wail, but they just held tight to the sides of the boat or to one another, with their eyes brimming with tears and their lips pressed tightly together. Except for Lucie and Elsebeth, who gazed up at him. There was fear in their eyes, but joy in their smiles. *No smiles yet, girls. Not until we're out of these woods.*

The water began to bubble and sing along the side of the boat as they sped along. Rudi was in front, so he pointed the way, extending his arm toward the notch in the western shore, where the lake poured out into a stream.

"Faster!" Marusch cried. Hansel looked over his shoulder and groaned. Rudi turned to see what the trouble was and drew in a sharp breath of rainy air.

A hundred yards behind them and closing fast was that rippling heap of water. *The murglin mother.*

The beast was many times faster than her offspring. The water rolled away from her exposed, arching back in cresting waves. Rudi could see the tiny forms of murglin babies clinging to her hide. Some of them squeaked, either frightened or excited. The mother's head began to rise, revealing bulbous eyes as big as Rudi's fists.

"She'll catch us before we get there!" Hansel shouted. Marusch realized it too. She stowed her pole by her side and reached for the bow she'd stashed at her feet.

It seemed like a miracle when Rudi plunged his pole again into the lake and found shallow water. It was waist deep now, instead of ten feet to the bottom. "Marusch, she won't be able to follow! It's not deep enough!" he shouted.

Sure enough, the murglin mother slowed. But she did not stop. Two enormous paws, both webbed and clawed, reached into the shallows, and she heaved herself up, plodding toward them on short, bowed legs. Her brood sensed danger. They sprang off her back like frogs and plinked and plunked into the water. The mother unleashed a horrible bubbling roar. Even at the prow of the boat, Rudi felt a humid blast of stinking hot air. He turned to glimpse a gargantuan head with fleshy barbs like a catfish, and a toothy jaw vast enough to swallow a person whole.

Before the beast got any closer, the wave that she'd created washed ahead of her and lifted the boat, propelling it even faster toward the gap that was now just twenty yards away—a gap too thin for the murglin mother's massive head. Hempel roared with delight, and Hansel reached over to tap Rudi's shoulder with his fist.

They slipped through the gap and into the stream. Just ahead on the right was a rock, as tall and wide as a castle door. It leaned over the water like a sagging headstone. As they neared it, Rudi's smile vanished and his blood ran cold. There was a faint red glow behind the rock, like the aura of the rising sun. "What is that?" he whispered.

The glow's intensity grew, and tiny winking lights rose up from behind the rock. They looked like the fireflies of early summer nights, except the color was wrong. Instead of a soothing white tinged with green, these were the color of light shining through a vial of blood. They circled around a tall, dark, slender shape: the shape of a man. But it was distorted somehow. He was too tall, too thin, too long-limbed, like a shadow cast by the setting sun. His spidery arms rose to stretch wide, and they ended in long-fingered hands with knifelike nails. A sodden, oily robe of thin material clung to his emaciated limbs.

Vilikus! Rudi heard the shrieks of the children, and he knew they'd seen him too. They covered their eyes and flattened themselves at the bottom of the boat. Hempel went on propelling the craft, gritting his teeth and growling with every push. Hansel gawked at the warlock. Marusch hunched over, either hiding or reaching for something at her feet.

Rudi could see the warlock's face now as the boat drew near. He wanted to look away, but found himself mesmerized instead.

The warlock's face was narrow and long, with a high forehead and a chin that tapered to a point. Only a few wisps of white hair clung to the sides of his head. His skin was like an onion's, thin and nearly transparent, so that the bones of his cheeks and jaw and the dark muscle and spidery purple veins could all be seen. And his shriveled, sunken eyes were the most horrible of all: dark red in the middle and an infected, blood-streaked yellow all around.

Hempel shuddered and hid his face, neglecting to drive the boat forward. Vilikus raised his arms. They spread horribly, inhumanly wide, and they creaked when they moved. His long sleeves hung down nearly to the rock, and he looked like a terrible bird about to take flight.

Then Rudi heard the warlock's voice. It was dry and whispery and should have been too quiet to perceive, but somehow Rudi heard it. It seemed like the words hissed right into his ear: "Hansel—is that you at last? And you, boy: you must be Rudiger . . ."

How? How can he know me? A scream caught in Rudi's throat, and he would have choked it out had the warlock said another word. Beside him Hansel stared up, petrified and white faced. But Marusch stood among the cowering bodies, notched an arrow in the string of her bow, and let it fly through the air. It hit the warlock in the chest, and twanged there, as if it had struck the hard wood of a tree instead.

The boat swept under the warlock's outstretched arms. A wicked grin spread across his face as he looked down on them. He reached for the feathered end of the arrow and Rudi watched, astonished, as he drew the shaft out. There was a wrenching, rasping sound as the arrow came out clean and bloodless, and Rudi saw a fine gray powder spill off the end. Vilikus examined the arrow with a satisfied smile while some of the fireflies circled it to illuminate it for him.

They were beyond the warlock now, still gaining speed as the stream quickened. Hempel was poling again with the strength of the terrified, and Marusch lay down her bow to help him.

Rudi's head spun with questions. *How could the arrow not have harmed the warlock? Why didn't he even bleed? Why had Vilikus done nothing to keep them from escaping?* Rudi thought he'd bring some terrible spell down on their heads, or send a swarm of murglins after them. But they'd simply floated out of the lake and into the forest. Now they just had to push the boat as fast as it could go, far away from the vile warlock and his servants. He looked back in time to see the dim glow of the fireflies fade from sight.

"Watch your heads!" Hansel cried. Rudi's heart leaped in his chest. He whirled around, expecting the worst. But it was only a thick, dead branch that sagged low across the river. Its bark had fallen away, and the wood below shone smooth and pale. They all bent low, and passed easily underneath.

Elsebeth raised her head, like a mouse peering from its hole. She looked at Rudi first and then the woods gliding by on both banks. "Have we done it? Rudi, are we safe?"

"Maybe, Elsie," Rudi replied. He squeezed her shoulder and rubbed the top of Lucie's head. A great relief swept over him, so powerful it made him dizzy. "Maybe."

The current alone would have moved them at a walking pace, but they used their poles anyway. Hansel finally paused to rub an aching shoulder, and Rudi was glad—

he didn't want to be the first to stop. He heard Marusch behind him: "Hempel, you should rest too."

"Not me." Hempel said this louder than he had to, and Rudi could tell the words were aimed at him.

"Where are we going?" his uncle asked.

"Away from the warlock. That suits me," Marusch replied.

"It's so dark," Rudi said. The fine rain still fell, but they'd left the glow of the cloud behind them. Rudi leaned forward and peered into the blackness.

"What do you see, little cousin?" Hansel said.

"I think maybe the stream's getting wider."

And it was. Until then the banks had been close and their branches sometimes scraped the sides of the boat. Now they retreated into the darkness. The chirps and croaks of insects and frogs grew faint with distance. Though he couldn't see, Rudi's senses told him they'd floated into a pond that was at least twenty yards across, maybe more.

"It's too deep for the pole," Hempel said. He'd pushed it down so far that even his hand was underwater.

"Then rest and see where the current takes us," Marusch told him. "Quiet, everyone. So we can hear if anything is following us."

The children had huddled low in the boat all this while, and many had fallen asleep. A few little heads popped up to peer around. The boat was spinning gently from Hempel's last push. Or at least, Rudi thought they were spinning. There was no way to be sure in the utter darkness. *I wish the stars would come out,* he thought. Then he'd know which way they were heading. He couldn't wait to see those points of diamond light again, to know they were out from under the warlock's mist.

He held his breath to listen as carefully as possible. But there were no sounds of pursuit that he could hear.

Rudi began to worry that this wide, still pond was as far as the boat would take them. Then he sensed the craft moving again. He put his hand in the water and smiled as he felt it ripple against his skin. "Marusch, the current is getting faster," he called back.

"Good," she said. Rudi heard the sound of little hands clapping behind him, and a few soft cheers.

The boat began to move so quickly that poling seemed unnecessary. *The faster the better. We're really going to make it,* Rudi thought. He used his pole only to fend them away from the banks, which had begun to close in again, branches clawing the sides of the boat.

The children whispered excitedly to one another about mothers and fathers and their own soft beds. A small voice piped up, louder than the others. "Rudi?"

Rudi squinted, but could see nothing. "Which one of you is that?"

"It's Lena. Was my father with you? Didn't he come with you to rescue us?"

No answer occurred to Rudi; he could only picture Tobias and the other fathers running pell-mell into the forest, to escape the phantom that Hansel had conjured. Rudi began to stammer, but felt a touch at his shoulder—Hansel's hand.

"Lena, dear, your father is very brave," Hansel said. "Children, all of your fathers tried to come. But a terrible creature got in their way. None of them were hurt, though. So don't worry. You'll see them soon."

Thank you, Hansel, Rudi thought.

For a long time the boat practically steered itself. Rudi's head drooped and his eyelids fluttered. But they snapped open wide when he heard Hansel shout, "Lower your heads!"

Again they all ducked. And as Rudi passed under the low-hanging branch, he saw that it was smooth and pale. He saw it, because there was light again within the cloud. "Something's wrong," he whispered.

Marusch sensed it too. She stared at the cloud and over the side of the boat, where the current had quickened even more.

"What?" Hansel said in a high, cramped voice. "What is it?"

"I think that was the same branch," Rudi said. "The one we passed before." A prickly heat swept across his face.

"That's not possible," said Hansel. He chuckled nervously.

Rudi squeezed his eyes half closed. He moved his hand as if stirring something with one finger. "We were spinning on that pond—we could have turned around. . . ."

"But a stream can't flow two ways!" Hansel cried.

"Water is his element—you told us that," Marusch said.

Please let this be a nightmare. It was too strange and terrible to be real. "We're going back! Back to *him*! We have to turn around!" Rudi shouted. He drove his pole into the water and stabbed at the soft bottom. Hansel did the same thing beside him. The pole bent in Rudi's hands, and he felt the tip scrape along the streambed. Finally the stern began to pivot around. When the boat was sideways, Hempel and Marusch had to raise their arms to fight off the branches that scratched at them.

"Push, everyone!" Marusch called once the boat had turned completely. But the stream tugged them backward, no matter how hard they worked.

Rudi turned. "No!" he shouted. The slanted stone was just ahead. And the red points of light rose once more to swarm around a towering, skeletal figure with his arms raised high and the sleeves of his robe flapping beneath like demon wings.

The stream surged. White waves frothed and splashed over the prow. In a moment half the distance between them and Vilikus had vanished. "Head for the shore!" Rudi shouted.

Hansel leaned over to Rudi's side and helped him push the boat toward the bank of the stream. Rudi heard him mutter "This can't be happening" over and over again.

Elsebeth leaned over the side and paddled with her

cupped hand. Behind her, Fye and Hendrik did the same, splashing furiously. The boat neared the shore, where a dense thicket grew, and Rudi and Hansel reached out from the prow to seize a branch with two hands.

Rudi heard Elsie scream. A slender, slick-skinned arm had risen out of the water and grabbed her wrist. It tugged at Elsie, threatening to pull her over the side. Lucie hugged her sister around the waist to keep her in the boat.

Murglin! Rudi let out a guttural cry and reached over the side. He hammered at the arm with his fist. But two more pairs of sleek gray hands shot up. They gripped the side of the boat and pulled it down. The far side of the craft lifted out of the water, and the powerful current surged underneath and tipped it sideways. Elsebeth tumbled out, dragged by the murglin.

Rudi shouted her name and dove after her. Before he plunged into the deep black stream, he heard the earsplitting sound of the other children shrieking as one. Then the water muted all the sounds to a dull aquatic roar.

In front of him Elsebeth bubbled out an underwater scream. Rudi took her hand, but something pulled at her from the other side. He reached past Elsie and struck at the murglin. He wanted to hurt the creature, to make it let her go, but the water slowed his fist and the blow slid harmlessly off the slick flesh. The murglin's tail lashed him across the head, and Elsebeth slipped out of his grip. He groped at the place where she'd been, but there was nothing but a watery void.

Rudi's lungs raged at him, commanding him to breathe, and he had to kick for the surface. He came up gasping. "Elsie!" he cried. He twisted his head to look in every direction, and he saw that the current had swept him all the way to the jutting rock.

The warlock loomed overhead, surrounded by a storm of winking crimson lights. Rudi heard his thin, ghastly voice. "Rudiger, Rudiger, did you think escape would be so easy?"

Rudi floated past the warlock, too stunned to do anything else. *How? How does he know me?* The current swept him into the lake, and Vilikus smiled down at him—a terrible smile with just the four middle teeth of his lower jaw remaining, and only the sharp dog teeth above.

Rudi tore his eyes away from the warlock and looked back at the boat. It floated backward, not far behind him. Marusch was gone—fallen in, probably. Hansel and Hempel were together at the prow. Hempel had a murglin by the throat and shook it like a rag doll. As the boat swept past the rock, three more of the creatures ran up beside Vilikus and hopped down into the craft, landing noisily among the screaming children. Hempel threw the senseless murglin over the side. He stepped between the newcomers and Hansel and raised his fists.

He's protecting Hansel, Rudi realized. Hansel had

Hempel's ax and lifted it to strike—but not at the murglins. He'd taken the Illusion Stone from around his neck and put it on the seat of the boat. *He's trying to destroy it!*

The ax came down upon the stone. There was a sound like a hammer striking a bell.

Hempel had two more murglins in his grasp, but the other slipped by him and seized the ax that Hansel raised for the second time. Hansel grabbed the stone by its chain and jumped off the boat. The murglin went in after him. A moment later Hempel stumbled and fell overboard as well, pulling his foes with him.

The boat drifted into the relative calm of the lake, with only terrified children inside. Rudi saw Lucie stand and scream. "Elsie! Elsie!"

Where are you, Elsebeth?

The current pushed him into something. Lines of crisscrossed rope. *A net,* he realized. *They're catching us like fish.*

Where are you, Elsie?

Lucie?

Marusch?

Hansel?

Uncle?

CHAPTER 15

Rudi choked and sputtered as murglin hands dragged him out of the shallows and cast him facedown onto a muddy shore. The muck got into his eyes, but he couldn't wipe it away because his arms were quickly lashed together behind him. He heard moans and cries all around him.

"Elsie! Lucie! Are you here?"

"I'm here," he heard Lucie say.

"So am I." Elsebeth sniffed, a little farther off.

At least she's alive, Rudi thought. That was the only good thing amid all this chaos and despair.

The murglins led Rudi, still blinded by the mud, into a boat. He tilted his face toward the sky so the rain might wash his eyes, but the drops were too fine and slow. He heard Hansel in the boat with him, and some of the children, and he sensed the others in another craft alongside them.

When he heard the sound of wood rubbing against

wood, he knew they'd reached a dock. Rudi was hauled out of the boat along with the rest. He felt wooden boards under his feet, then familiar, stony ground. *We're back at the prison island*, he thought.

One murglin held him by the shoulders while another untied his hands. Rudi shuddered at the slick, cool touch of the murglin's paw. Still blind from the mud, he was shoved into a crowded room. Strong arms saved him from stumbling. "I've got you, Rudi," Hempel said. "I'm so glad you're alive."

The door slammed behind them, and then came the thump of the heavy wooden bar dropping into place on the other side.

"Is there water here? I can't see!" Rudi cried.

A small hand took him by the arm. "Over here," he heard Elsebeth say. She led him to the side of the room, where a trough of water was against the wall. He filled his cupped hands, brought them to his eyes, and blinked into the fluid.

He could see again, though his eyes felt gritty and scratchy, and it burned when he blinked. There was some light from above, and he was surprised by the strange ceiling that covered the prison. The glowing cloud could be seen through a grid of bars that allowed the misty rain to penetrate.

"Is everyone here?" he said, prying mud from his ear with his little finger.

"Except Marusch," Hempel said in a wounded voice.

"Marusch? Did anyone see what happened to her?" Rudi asked the children who crowded around them. They shook their heads. He didn't know if he should be afraid that she'd drowned or hopeful that she'd escaped.

Hansel slumped in a corner of the room. Rudi knelt beside him and lowered his voice so no one else could hear. "I saw you try to destroy it. Were you able?"

Hansel shook his head. "Didn't even scratch it. It's as hard as a diamond." He looked toward the square opening in the door, then up at the grid in the ceiling, before leaning closer to Rudi's ear. "I dove to the bottom of the lake. Found a rock and put it underneath."

Rudi nodded. *But I'll tell Vilikus where to find it if he'll spare the girls,* he thought, blushing with guilt. *Sorry, Hansel.*

"I don't want it to rain anymore," Lucie moaned. She tugged at Rudi's shirt. "I'm cold."

Rudi put his arm around her. "I know. I wish I could build a fire for you." He patted the pocket of his pants and was surprised to find he hadn't lost his flint and steel when he fell into the lake. It wasn't much use here, though. The rest of his tinderbox with the charred linen and bits of grass and twig was in his pack, and he'd left that hidden by the shore. But even if he'd had those things, and wood to build a fire, the fine rain that filtered endlessly through the grate would have doused any flame.

He wished he'd remembered the steel in his pocket sooner, though. If he'd slipped that flat oval ring of metal over his fingers, he'd have packed a better punch against those vile murglins.

A sound from outside sent a cold chill into his heart. It was like trees rubbing together in the wind, or grindstones meshing. Rudi had heard the sound once before, when Vilikus raised his arms. This time it was rhythmic—the *screek, screek* of his bones as the warlock strode toward them, growing louder with each beat. The children knew what it was; they wailed and ran to the far side of the prison room, away from the door. Hansel drew his knees up to his chest where he sat, and Hempel stood with his fists bunched at his sides.

The creaking ceased. "Rudiger," said a rasping voice. Rudi saw Vilikus's long and narrow face, framed by the square hole of the prison door.

Rudi took three steps back. "I . . . I don't understand. . . . How do you know me?"

"I make it my concern to know things, Rudiger. Come to the door now. There is something I want you to witness. Perhaps Hansel should see this too. And that dull-witted uncle of yours. Come, the three of you." None of them moved. A wide and unpleasant smile curled up on the warlock's face. "Isn't one of your party missing? Don't you want to see what's become of her?" He brought his hand up to the square. It held Marusch's diamond pendant.

Rudi didn't want to go, but he had to know. His arms and legs trembled as he approached the door. He heard

Hansel and Hempel close behind him. Vilikus stepped away from the opening and Rudi peered through. Hansel leaned over his left shoulder, and Hempel his right.

The lake was in front of them. It shimmered under the glowing cloud. In the deepest part, between them and the dam, a boat moved across the water. In it were a pack of murglins and Marusch. She sat in the middle with spears aimed at her from the front and back. There was a tiny raft in the lake, and the boat pulled alongside it. Prodded by the murglins, Marusch stepped onto the raft. It was so small that another person couldn't have stood beside her, and it teetered as she shifted her feet to keep her balance.

"What are you doing with her?" Rudi cried out. Vilikus gave no answer. Hansel's hand closed on Rudi's shoulder.

The water churned a stone's throw away from Marusch, and then that moving mass of water headed toward her. Rudi saw the murglin mother's thick tail sweep from side to side to propel her great bulk forward. For a moment her enormous glossy eyes broke the surface. Then, when half the distance between them was gone, the beast arched her back and dove. The mound of water flattened out, and a cresting wave rolled out in a widening ring.

"Please, no," Hansel said.

Rudi watched Marusch lean out, trying to see the monster in the depths. She tensed and crouched, and at the last moment seemed to relax, as if she knew there was nothing she could do, unarmed and stranded on a flimsy raft.

The murglin mother exploded out of the water beneath her. The raft was shattered, and Marusch soared into the air and tumbled. The monster opened her jaws wide. Water streamed out from between her teeth as she waited for Marusch to tumble out of the sky.

Rudi spun around, unable to bear it. But he heard a woeful scream, suddenly cut off, and saw the horror in Hansel's expression. Hempel crumpled to the floor as if he'd been struck in the stomach. Rudi crushed his face against Hansel's chest.

On the other side of the door, he heard the warlock speak to his servants. "Bring the boy to me. Leave the others where they are. I will tell you soon enough what to do with them."

Rudi walked in a daze across the bridge to the tower island, surrounded by murglins on all sides. He stared at the ground as he trudged forward. His chest and head felt like they'd been hollowed out and scraped clean. He was vaguely aware that it was getting brighter. Somewhere to the east, beyond the stifling mist, the sun was rising.

The tower was before him, a rounded heap of gray slab, sweaty with water droplets that gathered and trickled down into the seams and cracks. At its foot there was an open door of thick black wood, held together by wide bands of rusted iron. Rudi was shoved across the threshold, and three of the murglins followed him in with spears leveled at his back.

Inside, Vilikus stood before a tall throne carved out of rock. Beside him a half-grown murglin leaped to its feet. The tiny thing pattered across the floor. It circled behind Rudi, then raced between his legs and back to its place beside the warlock. It stared at Rudi with its head tilted quizzically and its undeveloped arms folded in front like a mantis.

Rudi saw for the first time how tall Vilikus really was; he would even tower over Uncle Hempel. Rudi had to crane his neck to look at him.

"You're afraid of me," Vilikus said.

Rudi wasn't so sure that was true. He was too numb with grief to be afraid for himself. But there was one thing he was feeling for sure. He glared at the warlock.

"Hatred! Loathing!" Vilikus said. "I can see it in your eyes, Rudiger. That is fine. Those are virtues here." The warlock raised his arms in a sweeping gesture. "But tell me, what do you think of my home?"

Rudi glanced around. The gloomy room occupied the entire bottom of the tower. On one side of the throne, half the space was filled with barrels, stacked seven high. On the other side was a narrow wooden table with a single chair at its head. And in the center of the room was a wide, flat stone that rose hip high off the floor. Even in his somber daze, Rudi wondered about its purpose. It was the size and shape of a long bed, but with a deep oval basin carved out of the middle.

Rudi felt the misty rain on his face even here. He looked up. Overhead, between this and the rooms above it, there was no solid ceiling—just a grate like the one over the prison room. It rested on heavy timbers that spanned the tower and supported the stone walls. The rooms above, each with a grate for a ceiling and floor as well, could be reached by a staircase that hugged the curving walls.

He'd seen enough. *What do I think of this place?* Rudi just stared at the warlock with narrowed eyes.

"So angry," the warlock said. He waggled his fingers. The joints screeched with every move. "Because of what happened to Marusch, I suppose. That was her name, wasn't it? Was she important to you? She put an arrow in me, you know. She tried to *kill* me. It was futile, but she tried."

Rudi slipped his hands into his pockets so the warlock wouldn't see them shake. His fingers closed around the flint in one pocket and the steel in the other.

"You don't want to talk?" Vilikus cooed. "Perhaps you will feel differently when you see the surprise I have for you." The warlock turned toward a wooden crate as big as a coffin next to him. He lifted it effortlessly and heaved it toward Rudi, so that it landed smoothly on the stone floor and slid to a stop in front of him. Rudi was amazed that there could be such strength in the warlock's spidery limbs.

Vilikus extended a long finger toward the crate. "Raise the lid, Rudiger. It's a gift. I wish us to be friends."

Friends? Rudi almost laughed out loud. But he was afraid that if he started, the laugh would turn to a scream.

"Open it," the warlock commanded. Beside him the tiny murglin opened its mouth wide and gurgled at Rudi.

The sharp point of a murglin's spear prodded Rudi between his shoulder blades. He stepped over to the box. He flipped open the latch. Then he slipped his fingers under the edge of the lid, held his breath, and lifted.

CHAPTER 16

It was the purest, most unexpected moment of joy Rudi had ever known, and it exploded from him in a great whoop that echoed off the slabs of stone.

"Marusch! Marusch!" He leaned into the box and hugged her. Her arms and legs were bound, and she'd been gagged by a strip of cloth. She sat up, and Rudi fumbled at the knot of her gag and undid it, laughing and crying at the same time. "I can't believe it!"

Marusch spat out the cloth. "You can't believe *what?*"

"We saw what happened to you, Marusch! I can't believe you're not—" Rudi froze. Then he turned. He knew exactly what it all meant, and what he would see.

The grinning warlock swung the Illusion Stone back and forth by its chain. A smaller cloud of fireflies broke away from the rest of the swarm to swirl around the crude gem. "Yes, Rudiger. You can't believe your eyes anymore. The Simulapis is mine again. My murglins found it easily enough at the bottom of the lake. How I have missed it; how good it feels to wield it again."

Vilikus clasped his hand around the stone, and in the next instant a giant knight in twinkling silver armor stood before Rudi and Marusch. It was the same illusion that Hansel had conjured, but less ghostly and more genuine, like a true living thing. And Rudi noticed something else: When Vilikus conjured an illusion, it could be *heard* as well as *seen*.

The knight's armor squeaked as he turned to Vilikus, dropped to one knee with a clang, and bowed his head. He offered his sword, holding it by the blade with the handle extended toward the warlock.

Vilikus nodded, as if pleased with the tribute. He raised his other hand, splayed his spindly fingers wide, and then slowly closed them into a fist. The knight dropped the sword and lurched to his feet, and his armor began to crumple. Rudi saw the impressions of enormous unseen fingers on the chest and belly and legs. The phantom fingers bent and crushed the crinkling, screeching metal as the warlock tightened his imaginary grip. The knight floated off the ground as if the invisible hand lifted it. And as the armor was crushed, the knight jerked and twitched and began to shrink, until he was the size of an ordinary man.

Vilikus unclenched his hand, and the ruined knight clattered to the ground. His head landed near Rudi's feet, and the visor fell open. Rudi opened his mouth, but clapped a hand over it before a scream escaped.

Hansel's face was inside the helmet. Dead eyes staring.

"It's not real," Marusch said.

"I know," Rudi whispered into his palm. Bile burned in the back of his throat.

Vilikus laughed. Cracks appeared in the stone under the knight, and the floor caved in. Rudi knew it wasn't truly happening, but he still edged back from the bottomless chasm that opened before him. He watched Hansel the Knight tumble lifelessly down, escorted by the falling chunks of stone, until it all vanished into the black abyss.

When Rudi blinked, the floor was back as it was. Vilikus pressed the stone against his desiccated lips and slipped the chain over his neck.

Rudi's legs felt weak. He sat on the edge of the box that Marusch was still sitting in and closed his eyes. "You have what you want," he said. "Why don't you just let us go?"

He heard the bones in the warlock's knees groan as Vilikus shifted. "But, Rudiger, that wasn't all I wanted."

Rudi shivered, thinking about the face behind the visor and the note in the tent that started this nightmare. "You mean Hansel? Let him be, will you? Please, just let us all go!"

The warlock tapped the ends of his long fingers together. "It's not about Hansel, Rudiger. It never was. It's about my Simulapis. And something else." He turned toward his murglins. "Take the woman to the others. Let them have their happy reunion."

The murglins gripped Marusch by the elbows and pulled her out of the crate. They dragged her out of the tower with her bound feet sliding across the stone floor. "Careful," she called back before she disappeared. Rudi nodded.

Rudi was alone with the warlock now at the bottom of the tower. Vilikus waved his hand, and a group of the fireflies left the warlock's orbit and drifted toward Rudi. They circled him so that he too was bathed in the red glow. "Sit," Vilikus commanded him.

Rudi lowered himself to the cold floor and sat with his legs tucked underneath him, tiny before the towering warlock. The little cluster of fireflies settled into a lazy orbit around his head.

Vilikus eased his lanky form onto the great stone chair. His tapered fingers extended over the ends of the throne's arms, and they moved while he spoke, his pointy nails tock-ticking against the stone as if he played some instrument.

"Maybe things are not as grim as you think for you and your friends," the warlock said hoarsely.

Rudi drew in a sharp breath and dared to hope.

"The illusion I made for you, of Marusch in the jaws of the she-murg? That could still happen. I could feed all your friends to the beast. But it doesn't have to be.

Perhaps we could come to some sort of agreement." Vilikus stopped his drumming. "You may have something else that I need, something apart from the Simulapis."

Rudi felt a new threat, unforeseen until now, growing in his heart. "What could we have?"

"I mean you alone, Rudiger."

Rudi couldn't imagine what the warlock was talking about. He blinked nervously.

"I know what you're thinking," Vilikus said. He practically sighed the words. "What could a boy offer a mighty warlock? But there is something. Something I have missed for too many years." He leaned forward. "A companion, Rudiger. This is my offer: I will spare all the others, and let them go free. *If you promise to stay.*"

Rudi clutched his shirt. He tried to speak twice before the words finally escaped. "Me? No—no! I've heard about what you've done to your companions before—to your own daughter!"

"My daughter?" Vilikus grinned. "You mean the traitor I left behind on my island? That was not my true daughter. Nor was Ulfrida, the witch that Hansel and his sister met in these woods. Yes, I called them daughters, but once they were just children like you. Children whom my murglins stole for me, whom I thought showed promise. As *you* show promise, my boy."

The words were like a cold knife in Rudi's heart. "I . . . I show promise? You think I'm wicked like you?"

Vilikus leaned back and brought a hand to his face,

scraping the long nails along one cheek. Tiny flakes of skin fell like snow. "Wicked, you say? Evil is a matter of perception, Rudiger. Is a dog evil? So the cat believes. Is a cat evil? So the bird believes. Is a bird evil? So the worm believes. When you do what you do to survive, it isn't evil. It is the nature of the world. Evil is natural, Rudiger."

"But the things you do . . . how long you've lived . . . that isn't natural. It's unnatural. It's *supernatural*."

"Yes, Rudiger. How long I've lived. Perhaps I will share that secret with you. After all, is one lifetime really enough for you? In time everyone you know will be dead, and you will soon follow. Doesn't that make you angry? Doesn't everything about your poor, wretched life make you angry? I know it does, my boy. I know what rage runs through your veins. I know you better than you think. In fact, I've known about you for quite a while."

Rudi swallowed hard, but his mouth was dry and it pained his throat. "How could you know about me?"

"Would you like to see?" Without taking his eyes off Rudi, Vilikus extended his arm, palm up, and called out: "Join us, my dear."

There were footsteps overhead. Rudi looked up through the latticed ceiling and saw a dark figure in the room above. The figure came down the stairs, ominous and familiar. When he saw who it was, he thought his heart might cease beating.

Aunt Agnes.

CHAPTER 17

"Hello, little man. Are you surprised to see me?"

I shouldn't be, Rudi thought, and that was the worst of it. Hansel had told him that Vilikus used spies. Hadn't Agnes arrived at the same time the warlock must have come to the forest? And there were other signs, other terribly obvious signs. . . . "No," Rudi moaned. He couldn't stand to look at Agnes's smirking face, lit red by the fireflies as she took her place beside the warlock.

"Yes," Vilikus countered. If anyone else whispered in his ear that way, the breath would have been warm. But this was like ice. "Now you think you should have realized that Agnes was my servant. She came out of nowhere, didn't she? Why would such a lovely woman choose a feebleminded woodcutter for her husband? But there was a reason: Of course, I would place one of my spies in that village, in that *house*, if I was searching for

180

the stone. And I was wise to do so—it brought Hansel and the stone to me, did it not? Oh, but there's more, you're thinking. Abandoning the girls in the forest, for my murglins to find . . . did Agnes do that for me?"

"Of course I did," Agnes whispered in Rudi's other ear.

Rudi groaned, and squeezed his eyes shut. "Why didn't Uncle stop you? Why?"

He heard her laugh. "He tried, Rudi, he tried. It took a large dose of my master's potion in his dinner to weaken his resolve—a larger dose than usual."

Rudi winced as if he'd been kicked in the stomach. *Oh, Uncle, I'm so sorry. How could I know?*

He couldn't take any more. He prayed that they'd stop. But Agnes wasn't done. "And I wasn't just sending my master his dinner when I left those silly girls in the woods," she said. "I was stoking your ire, Rudi. I told Vilikus about you, what a promising young boy you were. How quick to anger!"

"Yes, Agnes told me what kind of boy you are. I was intrigued," Vilikus added. "So I told her to cultivate your anger, Rudiger. I said, 'Prepare him for me. Outrage him. Torment him.' Because that is how I want you, when we begin. That's the clay I mold, the canvas on which I paint. You see, Rudiger, I decided there were two prizes I could win in these woods. I could wield my Simulapis once more. And I could find a new companion to replace the witches who disappointed me."

Rudi's thoughts turned to chaos. He slumped forward and felt the warlock's impossibly long fingers clutch his shoulder to hold him up.

"It's all too much to take, isn't it, Rudiger? Your thoughts are tumbling out of control. *Good*. Let your mind crumble. I will put it back together for you, and it will be keener and fiercer than before. But first I need your answer. Do you agree—willingly—to stay, so the others may live?"

Rudi trembled, from his fingers to his toes. *You knew I would, you monster.* He nodded.

"There can be no breaking of this covenant, Rudiger. Know this: When little Lucie and Elsebeth return to the village, a tearful Agnes will be there, begging for another chance to care for them. And she will raise them, kindly enough."

"Master, no—," Agnes began, but Vilikus must have silenced her with a gesture.

"And if you dare to leave me, Rudiger, if you disappear from my side, the word will fly to Agnes. And she will put an end to those silly girls, and your hapless uncle, too. Won't you, Agnes?"

"*Oh, yes*," Agnes said. Rudi heard the glee in her reply.

"So tell me again," Vilikus whispered into his ear. "Do you agree to stay? With all your soul?"

Wake up, Rudi, he told himself, but he knew this was no dream. He opened his eyes, and there to his right was the warlock, orbited by those strange glowing bugs, and there to his left was Agnes, lovely on the outside but hideous within.

"Yes," he said in a breathless voice he barely recognized as his own. "I promise to stay. If you promise to let the others go."

Hansel, Hempel, and Marusch stood outside the tower, guarded by twenty murglins. Hempel had Marusch's hand clasped between his. Hansel wore a pale expression of utter sorrow, and he slumped as if a great weight pressed on his shoulders. The three of them stared, questioning, as Rudi stepped into the dim morning light.

Rudi walked directly to Hempel and threw his arms around his uncle. "I'm sorry for the way I treated you," he said. "You didn't deserve it, Uncle. You're a good man."

Hempel's bottom lip trembled. "I just wanted to make it up to you, Rudi."

Rudi wished he could tell Hempel more—about Agnes, about everything—but Vilikus had warned him. *I'll be listening*, the warlock said, and Rudi sensed him overhead, at one of the tower's slender windows. He glanced up and saw a single red point of light drift outside one of the dark slits, winking on and off.

"What's happening, Rudi?" Hansel asked. "What did Vilikus want?"

Rudi looked at each of them and finally turned his

eyes toward the rocky ground. "Vilikus will let you go. But I'm staying."

Hansel gasped.

"No!" Hempel cried.

Rudi raised his hands, palms out. How could he explain it? "Please. He won't . . . he's not going to . . . He wants me to be his companion. Don't try to talk me out of it. That was our bargain."

"A bargain with the devil," Marusch said.

"Yes," Rudi said. "But I had to make it. Either all of us would die, or all of us would live. What else could I do?"

"The fate you've chosen is worse than death, Rudi! You could end up like—like Ulfrida, for heaven's sake!" Hansel said.

"I made a promise to the girls, Hansel. I promised to keep them safe, no matter what. This will save them. And the rest of the children, and the three of you, too. So you can't tell me it wasn't worth it. Marusch, will you tell the girls good-bye, and that I love them?"

"Tell them yourself," Marusch answered, watching him with a steady gaze.

"I can't," Rudi said, choking out the words. "I couldn't bear it. Just say it for me, will you? It's the last thing I'll ever ask of you. Now go! And never come back for me. *Never.*"

"You can't do this—let the warlock take *me*!" Hansel said. He looked up at the tower and shouted. "Do you hear me, Vilikus? Take me instead!" He stepped toward Rudi, but found the point of a murglin's spear thrust between them.

Rudi couldn't talk anymore; his throat had tightened so much he could barely breathe. He waved them away and walked into the tower, with his vision blurred by tears.

CHAPTER 18

"It's strange," Hansel said. "I only had that little fellow by my side for a few days. Now it doesn't feel right without him."

Hansel, Hempel, Marusch, and the children rode in one of the murglins' boats. The adults were at the prow, the children in the middle, and at the rear, a single burly murglin propelled the craft with a long pole.

"Think that thing can understand us?" Hansel whispered.

Marusch nodded.

"Then I'll keep it quiet. Something is very strange about this," Hansel said.

"What's strange?" Hempel asked.

"Vilikus letting us go," Hansel replied. "It's not his way."

"I don't understand," Hempel said.

"He's a monster, Hempel. But he's not stupid. He knows we'll tell other people, and that's the last thing he wants, even if he has the Illusion Stone to protect him. So why let us go?"

Marusch looked at the murglin behind them, and the shore ahead. "He isn't letting us go," she said softly.

Hansel stared at her, wide-eyed.

"He wants Rudi to believe that," she said. "But you're right, Hansel. We're in danger. Now listen, both of you. . . ."

A pair of murglins, each armed with a spear, awaited them on the eastern shore, One took the lead and the other moved to the rear. "My servants will escort you," Vilikus had told them in his chilling voice. Hempel followed the lead murglin, the children were next, and then Marusch and Hansel. Their weapons were gone, of course: lost at the bottom of the lake, or seized by the warlock's servants.

The path from the shore led them up the slope. Before long, they walked over a stony ridge that brought them out of sight of the warlock's tower. Marusch peered into the woods, right and left. Hempel turned back to look at her, and she nodded.

Hansel clutched his stomach, groaned, and pitched over onto the ground. The murglin at the rear stared down at him curiously. Marusch lunged, surprising it, and grappled with the creature for its spear.

The lead murglin turned to see what was happening,

only to find that Hempel had crept close behind. Hempel seized the murglin's neck with one hand and plucked the spear away with the other.

At the rear of the line Hansel jumped to his feet and brought his fist down on the head of the murglin that Marusch wrestled. Marusch ripped the spear out of the stunned creature's hands. It stumbled back and hissed at them. Marusch leveled the spear at the creature. "Leave us! We need no guide! We'll find the way ourselves!"

The murglin gaped at her with its great glassy eyes. Then it turned and ran, letting out a long, gurgling cry that was answered by more of its kind, not far away.

"They're coming!" Marusch said.

"You were right, Marusch," Hempel said. He still had the other murglin by the neck, and he heaved the squealing thing into the underbrush. There was a half-dead tree nearby, and he wrenched a thick branch from the trunk with a loud *crack*. He handed the captured spear to Hansel and raised the branch like a club. "Now we have three weapons," he said, smiling.

Marusch looked at the woody landscape around them. Her eyes focused on the higher ground to their left, and a short but steep hill of rock that might be more easily defended.

"We can't outrun them. And we can't fight them here. Up to the heights!" Marusch said. "Go, children—as fast as you can!"

Hansel groaned and followed them. As they ran they could hear the slap of amphibious feet and the sound of branches snapping.

Vilikus leaned out from a high window of his tower. His hands on the sill looked like a pair of enormous white spiders.

Beyond the lake, forty of his most lethal murglins ran along the ridge on the eastern shore. Soon they would intercept Hansel and the rest of his defenseless group. And that would end this threat to the warlock's secrecy.

Agnes stepped behind him and touched his shoulder. "Forgive me, master. I thought you were serious when you said I had to return to that miserable house and tend to those horrible children."

Vilikus peered at her from the corner of his red eyes. "You should have known better, my dear. Nobody is allowed to see my lair and live. Except my beloved spies, of course."

She bowed her head and smiled at the compliment. "Have I served you well, master?"

"Perfectly, my dear. Like your parents before you, and your grandparents before them. But you have outdone them all; you have helped me recover my most valuable possession. Soon you may return to your true home, with a reward worthy of your service."

Agnes sighed happily. She looked out the window

toward the eastern shore. "What will you do to them?"

"My hunter murglins will track them down. The boy must never know, of course."

"He won't hear of it from me," Agnes said. She touched the back of the warlock's hand, and a fine dust came off on her fingers, like the powder on a moth's wing. "You need your oil, master," she said.

"So I do," Vilikus said. "Perhaps Rudiger's lessons can begin now."

"My legs hurt," Fye said. Without a word, Hansel scooped her up. When the other children saw him carrying her, they began to complain.

"You can all rest in a minute," Marusch shouted. "For now, pick up as many stones as you can carry!"

They scrambled up to the rocky outcrop where they would make their stand. She and Hansel herded the children in front of them. Hempel followed, snapping off more heavy branches and stacking them across his arms.

In the dead forest behind them, they heard the call of murglins. Marusch turned her ear toward the sound. "They've split into two groups," she whispered to Hansel. "They will close on us like pincers."

She was grateful at least that the murglins had no bows and arrows; those slimy fingers with their knobby ends weren't nimble enough for such an elegant weapon. It was spears and clubs for these creatures.

They stood at last at the highest point. Marusch

kneeled in front of the children. "Who here has a good strong arm to throw the stones?"

A few of the children raised their hands. "I threw an apple all the way over our barn once," Hendrik said.

"Very good, Hendrik. Those who can throw, throw. Those who can't, look for rocks and give them to the throwers—to Hempel especially. Little ones: stay behind the adults. We'll teach these murglins to fear the children of Waldrand, won't we?" The children nodded. Marusch glanced at Hansel. He smiled wearily and shrugged.

A rattling, bubbling war cry rang out from the woods on opposite sides of the hill. The murglins streamed out from between the trees. When she saw how many, Marusch closed her eyes and sighed heavily. A dozen they might have handled; twenty would have overwhelmed them. Here was twice that number, attacking from two sides.

"Pincers," Hansel said.

"Children, hold the stones until they're close," Marusch called out. Her voice betrayed no fear. She, Hansel, and Hempel formed a triangle around the children. The murglins came for them, charging up the hill.

Hempel found that one of the largest stones atop the outcropping was loose. He put his shoulder to it and heaved. The boulder rumbled down. It bounced higher as it went, over the head of one murglin and into the chest of another. "One less to worry about!" Hempel shouted, grinning.

"Now!" Marusch shouted.

They unleashed their stones. The creatures ducked and darted, but a few of the missiles found their marks. Hempel struck one hard between the eyes, and it toppled back and rolled down the hill. The others that were hit hissed menacingly and kept climbing.

When they ran out of stones, Hempel flung the heavy branches he'd collected. But it only slowed their advance. The murglins spread out around the entire hill and edged toward the gaps between Marusch, Hempel, and Hansel.

"We can't stop them!" Hansel cried. The first murglins had almost reached them. A dozen sharp spears stabbed upward, with three more waves behind them. Hempel drew the last, biggest stick over his shoulder like a club, and waited for them to take the final steps.

Hansel's spear shook as he jabbed at the shrinking space between him and the murglins. He clenched his teeth and winced. Then a piercing squeal erupted from one of the creatures below him. Its body thrashed in serpentine contortions that sent it tumbling down the hill.

Another murglin in front of Marusch screamed and lashed its tail in a frenzy. As it twisted, Marusch saw the feathered shaft of an arrow in the creature's back. Two more arrows clattered off the stones.

A voice called out from below: "Hempel—Hansel! Hold them off another minute!"

Lena had been huddled on the ground with the other

children, but leaped up when she heard the voice and waved her arms. "Father! I'm here, Father!"

The fathers of Waldrand were back: Tobias, Kurt, Oskar, Erwin, Nikolaus, Georg. And Burck was with them. They dashed out from the trees, stood at the bottom of the hill, and took closer aim with their bows.

The murglins hesitated, unsure of whether they should continue their assault or turn to fight the newcomers. Hempel roared and leaped down the slope. He swept his club from side to side, and three more creatures dropped. Marusch pierced another with her spear.

The rest of the army turned and ran down the slope. The air filled with the twangs of strings, the whoosh of arrows, and the animal squeals of wounded murglins. Finally the last of the creatures fell or ran or crawled into the forest. The children rushed down the hill and leaped into their fathers' arms, laughing and weeping. Tobias lifted Lena over his head. Kurt covered Fye's head with kisses. Hendrik had to tell Nikolaus that he was hugging too hard.

Hansel went to Tobias, offered his hand, and smiled. "Thank you. That's a miracle, you coming when you did."

Tobias shifted Lena so he could hold her with one arm and shake Hansel's hand. "No miracle. Burck picked up your trail, and that got us here. We watched for a while, arguing over what to do. Then you came out with the children, so we followed you." He turned to Hempel. "And how did you get here? I thought we left you behind in Waldrand. It's a good thing you didn't listen to us, my friend."

Hempel shrugged. "I just wanted to help."

"You must be brave folk," Erwin said, stepping up with his son in his arms. "You kept going, to save our young ones, even after that awful phantom appeared at the cottage. It took us a day to get our courage up again." Erwin glanced at Burck, who was some distance off, examining a dead murglin. He lowered his voice to a whisper. "Burck refused to come, until we threatened to tell the whole village he lost his nerve."

Hansel pursed his lips at the mention of the phantom. "Well . . . everyone's afraid at some time or other. . . ."

"They *are* brave—especially Marusch!" Lena cried. The fathers looked toward Marusch, who sat on a rock apart from the others. Burck lowered his head.

Tobias went to Marusch and kneeled in front of her. "Good woman, you've saved our children. Please accept our thanks and forgive our ignorance—if you can forgive the unforgivable."

Marusch nodded, keeping her face turned toward the ground.

"But wait," Tobias said. "One of you is missing. Where is Rudi?"

Marusch raised her head. "He traded his freedom— his very soul—for our lives. But the warlock lied; he meant to kill us all along. So the pact is broken."

The men exchanged worried looks. "What do we do now?" Tobias asked.

"You men, take the children home," Marusch said. "And Lucie and Elsebeth, too. Rudi would want to be sure they were safe. I will go back for him. All I ask is that you loan me a bow and a quiver full of arrows."

"I'm coming too," Hempel said. "So is Hansel."

Hansel raised his arms, palms up. "Why not?"

What's going to happen to me?

Rudi leaned against the chest-high wall on the top of the tower. The grate under his feet was slick with mist. He wiped the drizzle off his cheeks and wondered if he would ever feel dry again.

Vilikus and Agnes had left him alone, disappearing into a curtained room on the second floor. The warlock didn't seem to care if Rudi wandered. Still, the lone door out of the tower was shut and guarded, and the tiny murglin pattered behind him wherever he went.

The third story of the tower, just below him, was a library and a storehouse, with the warlock's collected knowledge of sorcery and other wicked arts. The books were wrapped in oilcloth to protect them from the omnipresent damp. There were dozens of chests and boxes, some already shut and locked, and others with their lids open, as if ready to be filled.

Now, atop the tower, Rudi saw the entire lake. The

dam was to the south. To the east the stream poured in, and to the west was the notch where it left. And to the north, which he hadn't seen well until now, there were more islets; one with a large, low windowless place, like a storehouse, and dozens of the domed heaps of sticks and mud where the murglins dwelled.

The most distant isle lay in this direction as well, a hundred yards away, with no bridge connecting it to the others. On it was a small stone building that was different from all the others on this lake. It had a solid roof, and a chimney. As Rudi watched, a stream of smoke emerged from the stack, and a warm orange glow appeared through the single window that he could see.

Behind him he heard the scrape of footsteps, each step rising in pitch. Someone was coming up the stairs. *Agnes.* Rudi's lip curled in distaste, and he turned back to stare at the distant isle.

He heard Agnes at his shoulder. "Vilikus commands you to go to him," she said.

Rudi pointed to the north. "What's that—where the smoke is?"

She glanced out at the lake, and scowled at him. "The kitchen. The ovens. What else would it be?"

"Ovens? Who cooks for him?"

"Murglins, of course."

Rudi looked at the isle again and furrowed his brow. "Why put the kitchen all the way over there? Not convenient, is it?"

Agnes opened her mouth to harangue him in a snarling gesture Rudi had seen countless times before. Then she calmed herself and grinned smugly.

"So headstrong! But now Vilikus has commanded you, and you must go to him. Remember, Rudi, you agreed to this bargain. You are his to command."

"Maybe I am, but why are you? Why do you help him?"

Agnes narrowed her eyes and smiled. "Why serve the great warlock? So that when my work is done, I can go home and live like an empress for the rest of my life. And I mean my *real* home, not that miserable pigsty of Hempel's. You see, little man, my family has served Vilikus for generations, and he has rewarded us handsomely. Do you realize how easily treasure came to him? All he had to do was use the Simulapis to make ships wreck themselves on the rocks around his island. Then his murglins retrieved the sunken gold. So there was plenty for him, and plenty for his spies. Now enough of your questions! Come with me, or learn the price of disobedience."

She walked down the stairs, and Rudi waited a moment before following in a small but deliberate show of defiance. The tiny murglin stretched its mouth wide and hissed at him as he walked by. Rudi fought the urge to seize it by the tail and sling it off the tower.

A strange sight greeted him as he came down to the first story.

The warlock was lying in the hollow oval of the

wide, flat stone, robe and all. The basin was already half filled with clear, fragrant oil, and a pair of stocky murglins poured in another barrel. Soon only Vilikus's narrow face was above the pool of oil. Some of the red fireflies hovered over the warlock. Others rested on the edge of the basin, surrounding him like a twinkling wreath.

Vilikus looked sideways at Rudi. "Ah, Rudiger. This is my regimen—one of the secrets to staying alive for all these centuries."

"*One* of the secrets?" Rudi asked.

"One, yes," Vilikus said. "Eating right is another." He flashed a predatory grin that made Rudi's stomach twist. "But you may learn all my secrets, if you are a faithful companion."

The murglins finished filling the basin. Rudi watched them carry the empty barrel out of the tower. "Maybe I don't want your secrets," he muttered.

"No? Who wouldn't want to live a thousand years?"

"Not me. Now that I've seen what it's done to you. You're a monster." Rudi knew his words were bold, but he didn't care about that or anything else anymore. The warlock seemed amused, not angered.

"It's true I'm not the man I was," Vilikus said. "I was a *warlord* before a *warlock*, you know. But think of the knowledge I've accumulated, Rudiger. For example, your friend Marusch. Poor, disfigured Marusch. Would it interest you to know there are others like her? Of course it would—you don't want it to show, but I see the look in your eyes.

"Yes, Rudiger, Marusch is not unique. It happens to people now and then. An affliction—a mere sickness, like the pox—causes the sun to pain their eyes, peels back their lips, and stains their teeth red. There's nothing sinister about it, but the ignorant folk of the world think otherwise. The Marusches are shunned and persecuted. Their own families cast them out. They're called ghouls or vampires, when they're nothing of the sort!" The warlock smiled and laughed softly. "Isn't that the most delicious thing you've ever heard? And you call *me* a monster."

Vilikus closed his terrible red eyes and slid down along the curve in the stone, submerging completely. Rudi leaned closer and saw the long, ghastly face through inches of clear oil. A bubble floated out of the warlock's nose and rose up slowly like a silver pearl. His hands came together at his chest, and Rudi saw that he held the seeing stone, and caressed it with his fingertips. The warlock's eyes opened slowly, and Vilikus stared up from under the oil with his face distorted by the ripples.

Rudi felt a chill in the marrow of his bones. His heart pounded, and he felt suddenly dizzy. He pushed himself away from the stone and staggered back.

What have I done? he asked himself.

What you had to do, the answer came. *And it was worth it. You saved them all. Elsie and Lucie are safe.*

He wondered about that, though. The ovens were lit, not an hour after the warlock set them free. *What does he mean to cook?*

CHAPTER 19

Hansel rubbed his eyes and looked out again. A hundred yards away, the things were still there.

"Illusion or not?" Marusch said.

"Can't tell," said Hansel. He peered from behind the boulder again.

Murglin giants surrounded the perimeter of the dark lake.

If Hansel stood next to one, he didn't think he'd come up to its elbows. They were brawny, awesome things, like slick-skinned, wingless dragons reared up on two legs. Barbed tongues flickered out of mouths that were filled not with the needlelike teeth of the murglins they'd seen, but gleaming rows of six-inch ivory daggers. They had bulging black eyes like the murglins, but with vertical yellow slits in the middle. Their weapons were not spears, but massive clubs with thorny heads.

Hansel turned his back to the boulder and leaned against it. His face was pale. "You have to admit, Vilikus is clever. It's another breed of the creatures we've already met. So we can't be sure if they're real or not."

"If you ask me," Marusch said, "he's too clever for his own good. If he'd conjured a thousand normal murglins instead, we'd have been fooled for sure—how could we tell the illusions from the real thing? But Vilikus is arrogant. He had to show off something more terrible."

"You're the clever one, Marusch," Hempel said. He put his hand on her arm and gently squeezed.

Marusch shot him an inscrutable look, squeezing one eye half closed. She shook her head to clear her thoughts. "They *are* illusions," she said. "They have to be. Or we would have seen them before."

"I know that. My heart knows it, anyway," Hansel said. "But my eyes aren't so sure. And my legs have their doubts."

"I will go," Marusch said, though even she trembled at the thought. "I will close my eyes." She picked up the bow that Tobias had loaned her and rose to her feet.

Hempel pulled her back. "No. Let me. If something happens, you may still be able to help Rudi. This is something I can do."

Marusch put her hand over Hempel's and squeezed it.

Hempel smiled at her. "Tell Rudi what I've done. That I tried to help."

"You will tell him yourself," Marusch said.

Hempel shrugged. His own ax was long gone, taken by the murglins, but Oskar had left one for him to use.

He lifted the ax and waggled it, gauging the weight. "In case it's not an illusion," he said. And he stepped out from behind the boulder and walked toward the giants.

As soon as he was in the open, three of them turned Hempel's way. They strode toward him with their clubs raised over their heads. Marusch gripped Hansel's shoulder and squeezed hard enough to make him wince.

Their speed was awesome: Every stride put ten more feet of soggy earth behind them. A moment later they surrounded Hempel. The creatures opened their maws and hissed, with strings of pink drool dangling from their jagged teeth. Hempel raised the ax, holding it back over his shoulder, ready to strike the first giant to move closer.

They stood there, man and monsters, unmoving, except for the clubs that waggled in the air over the giant's heads. But they did not strike.

Hempel stepped forward. The giants hissed and moved back. He took another step, and again the giants retreated. He leaped forward and swung the ax at the nearest monster. It leaped back. Hempel looked back at his friends and shrugged. Then he brought the ax back over his head and flung it at the middle giant. Where it should have struck the creature, it simply vanished without resistance, but there was a soft thump as the ax struck the ground behind it.

"I think it's safe," he called back, grinning happily.

Marusch walked out from hiding, while Hansel hesitated behind the boulder. "I know they're not real, but

I'm still shaking," he said. He turned away as another pair of the monstrous illusions raced toward Marusch.

Marusch came back to him. "Put your hand on my shoulder, and I will lead you." And that is how they went. Hempel gawked at the giants with his ax over his shoulder, and Marusch led Hansel, who stared at the ground and used one hand to shield his eyes. The giants hissed at them, waved their clubs, and finally ignored them as they walked by.

The three crawled to the shore on their bellies across the damp, muddy ground. The lake was filled with murglins in boats—fifty craft or more, dispersed around the edge. They flattened themselves behind a stand of ferns when a small craft passed nearby, with one murglin propelling the boat and another scanning the shore. The creatures were so close, they could hear the murglins breathing and the water dripping off the pole.

"Vilikus must have heard about the failed attack," Hansel said when it was safe to speak. "They're watching for us."

Marusch nodded. "So many murglins. How will we get past them?"

"I know," Hempel said. They looked at him with raised eyebrows.

"Don't look so surprised," Hempel said, sounding wounded. "I get an idea every now and then."

"Tell us," Marusch said.

"Well . . . remember when we first saw the dam? There was a tiny leak, and it got the murglins crazy, trying to fix it. What if I put a huge hole in that wall?"

"Many of them would rush down to help repair it," Marusch said.

"Right!" Hempel said, smiling.

"So you're just going to walk up to the dam and hit it with your ax?" Hansel said.

"No, no," Hempel said, shaking his head vigorously. "There was one big tree still standing, close to the dam. I'll chop it down, and *crunch*! There goes the wall."

Hansel peered toward the southern end of the lake. He could see the upper edge of the dam, a vein of mud and pointed sticks rising above the flat, still water. Beyond that, he saw the upper branches of the tree that Hempel meant to topple.

"There are murglins on the wall, Hempel," Hansel said. "They'll come after you."

Hempel's shoulders rose and fell. "Not before I take that rotten old tree down."

"You would do this?" Marusch said in a quaking, halting voice.

"For Rudi I would," Hempel said. "It will be dark by the time I get there. You two stay here. You'll know when it's your time to go." He paused, and a worried look darkened his face. He ran his hand from his forehead to his chin, as if wiping that expression away. And he smiled. "So long then, Hansel. Good-bye, Marusch."

CHAPTER 20

Hempel crept around the shore, from the high eastern ledge to the low swampy ground before the dam. He stayed far enough from the water to avoid being seen by the patrolling murglins, but not so far that he attracted the attention of the gigantic illusions that stalked the forest. Night was coming, and again the dim glow of the cloud cast the only light.

He crawled behind a fallen trunk and peeked out at the dam. There was a murglin on the wall not too far away, another farther down, and another in the distance, barely visible. They were keeping watch on the perimeter. Hempel saw the tree they'd hidden behind when they first arrived. It was thick and tall but nearly dead, its roots drowned by the never-ending rain. Only a branch or two had leaves, and the rest were bare. It stood easily close enough to hit the dam if it fell in the right direction. He was pleased to see that it didn't lean in any particular direction; that made it easier to aim its fall.

And there was no breeze to worry about, or any trees nearby for its branches to tangle with; those were the things a woodcutter always considered. The question was: Could he fell *it* before the murglins felled *him*?

He ran his thumb along the edge of the ax blade and frowned. It was too dull for his liking. His own ax was sharp enough to whittle with. And this one was not as wide or heavy or long in the shaft.

When the closest murglin was looking the other way, he took a deep breath and stepped out from hiding. He moved swiftly and quietly toward the tree. When he reached it, he held the ax at arm's length to measure the distance, widened his stance, and swung it at a spot waist high on the side facing the dam.

Thwock! The first blow pierced the bark and sank deep into the rotted, spongy wood. The murglin's head snapped around and craned toward him.

Thwock! He swung the ax again. The murglin arched its head back and let out a long, gurgling cry. The other murglins that patrolled the dam came running.

"Yes, come on," Hempel cried with his lip curling high on one side. "All of you!" He swung furiously, and the bark and pulp flew. He cut downward and upward by turn, hacking a v-shaped notch in the trunk, a wide one that would not pinch and trap his blade when the tree began to sag. The rotted wood made the work go fast. The wedge was already a foot deep, and the ground was littered with chunks of soggy wood filled with wriggling termites.

When he brought the ax back again, he saw the nearest murglin slither down the face of the dam. It descended headfirst, holding the narrow spear between its teeth and using its hands to grasp at the jutting sticks.

The murglin reached the ground, stood, and rushed at him. Hempel stopped his assault on the tree for a moment to face the creature. The murglin thrust the sharp point of the spear toward his belly, but Hempel turned it aside with the face of the ax, and brought the handle back to strike the murglin. The creature wailed and staggered away. Two more murglins had reached the ground, but having seen what happened to the first, they waited before attacking. Hempel returned to the tree, swinging madly.

Behind him the prow of one of the flat boats appeared at the top of the dam. A dozen murglins leaped out and scrambled down the wall.

There was little time left for Hempel now. Roaring like a lion, he hacked again at the tree as the murglins came for him, spreading out in a half circle. He'd sliced halfway through the trunk, so he leaped to the opposite side. He started a second notch there, behind and above the first cut. When the wood between the notches was too thin to support the tree, down it would go, right where he'd aimed it.

He hacked once, twice, three times. The murglins closed in.

"Not yet!" Hempel screamed, and he forced them

back with a great sweep of the blade. His ax bit into the tree once more, and he heard a deep groan from the trunk. A murglin darted forward and jabbed at him. The spear struck Hempel's thick leather belt, and he felt a stinging pain where the sharp point came through. He hurled the ax at the closest murglin and threw his back against the tree, pushing with his legs.

He growled as he heaved, and the roar turned into a name that he bellowed as loud as he could, even as the deadly points came closer.

"Rudi!"

CHAPTER 21

Hansel hid alone near the water's edge and gnawed at his fingernails.

"Let us split up," Marusch had told him. "One of us might be able to get to Rudi while the other's way is blocked."

It seemed like wisdom when she said it. But now, lying in the dark behind a rock as murderous beasts prowled the waters, every instinct told Hansel to get up and run until he'd left this lake, this rain, and these woods behind forever.

Marusch was somewhere to his right, the dam to his left. And suddenly things happened in both directions.

A pair of murglins in a boat near the place he imagined Marusch was hiding howled and pointed at the shore. They leaped into the waist-deep water to search among the rocks and underbrush. *Get away from her*, he thought. He clutched the ferns in front of him and held his breath.

And then, from the direction of the dam, Hansel heard

another gurgling cry. It was answered by a boatful of creatures that rushed to the dam and poured out of their craft. Then there was the faint sound of someone shouting. Hansel wasn't sure what the word was. Could it be *Rudi*?

The sound pierced his heart. He peered into the gloom, and saw, beyond the dam, the top of the tree wobble and fall. It plunged into the dam, and the wall buckled where it struck. The sound, a wrenching crunch, reached his ears a moment later. Ripples flowed away from the dam—and suddenly reversed themselves as water poured through the ragged hole where the tree had struck. The empty boat slid off the edge of the dam, drawn by the current. Hansel watched the craft float toward the breach, upend, and disappear over the far side.

"You've done it, Hempel," he said quietly. "Now get out of there."

Murglins shrieked, and boats from all over the lake turned and headed for the disaster. More of the creatures emerged from their domed dwellings, and leaped into the vessels moored nearby. He peered toward the right, hoping that the group stalking Marusch would depart as well, but bit his bottom lip when he saw the long flat boat pulled up on the rocks, and the murglins still on the shore, probing the tall grass with their spears.

The path to the tower was clear. He rolled onto his back and closed his eyes. "So it's up to me, is it? The greatest coward in the bunch," he muttered. He breathed in deeply, exhaled slowly, and crawled on his hands and knees down to the water, as wobbly as a newborn fawn.

"And where are you, mother murglin?" he whispered, scanning the lake for the beast. Except for the chaos at the dam, the surface was still.

He eased in on all fours, thankful that he knew how to swim. With as little of his head above water as possible, he headed for the tower island.

To the north he saw an island where smoke wafted from a tall chimney. *The warlock's ovens*, Hansel presumed. His thoughts leaped across time to another place, not far from this one, when he and his sister were prisoners of another villain with the same unspeakable appetite.

Sorry, Vilikus, he thought. *Your dinner is on its way back to the village.*

He looked again at the warm orange light. It seemed so out of place amid all this darkness and damp. Why put your kitchen on an island so far away, without a bridge to connect it? Ulfrida had her oven right in the cottage.

His heart began to thump wildly. *But Ulfrida didn't have your secret to immortality. And the rain has something to do with that, doesn't it, Vilikus?*

After all, why the rain? To fill the lake for your murglins? The stream will do that. To cloak you in mist? The Illusion Stone could have done that when you had it for all those centuries. That's not what the rain is for at all.

Is it?

CHAPTER 22

Rudi sat at one end of the long table, Vilikus at the other. A murglin loped into the room through the tower's only door, bearing a plate that he put before Rudi.

The warlock waved his fingers, and once again a small group of the fireflies left to swirl around the boy.

"What are these things?" Rudi asked, squinting and raising a hand to his face.

"Creatures I've bred to serve me," the warlock said, sounding bored. "To light my way."

"What's the matter with candles?"

Vilikus chuckled. "Agnes was right about you, Rudiger. You always have something to say."

Rudi looked down at his plate. On it were three headless eels and a slice of a monstrous gray mushroom. He was torn between heartsickness and hunger, and hunger won. Just barely. He peeled the charred skin off an eel, pinched off a chunk of the white flesh, and popped it into his mouth. It was cooked, but cold.

The warlock leaned forward and stared at Rudi as if he was a curiosity at the village fair.

"You're not eating?" Rudi said.

"This is not to my taste," Vilikus said, smiling.

Rudi leaned back in his chair and covered his face with his hands.

"This sorrow will move on in time," Vilikus said, lacing his fingers together. And after a pause, he added, "And so shall we."

Rudi looked out from between his fingers. "What do you mean?"

"We will leave these woods, Rudiger. Forests vanish in time; men forever peck away at their edges, whittling them down until nothing is left. I prefer islands."

"But how . . . ," Rudi stammered.

"You wonder how we can move without being seen? The same way we traveled here. The cloud follows us and cloaks us. The murglins carry my possessions, and the she-murg bears the heaviest things. And now that the Simulapis is mine again, the journey becomes easier. No one would dare to approach us."

Rudi felt the last bit of warmth drain from his face. He pushed the plate away. Whatever appetite he'd mustered was gone. "When?" he said.

"Very soon," Vilikus replied.

While Vilikus went to his library to fill his crates with books, Rudi wandered back to the top of the tower.

Standing outside made him feel a little less imprisoned.

Overhead the spinning mist cast its pale silver light on the lake. *Somewhere up there, the moon is shining*, he thought. He supposed the day would come when he wouldn't remember what the moon looked like. It would be forgotten, along with the sight of the dusty light of the Milky Way across the night sky, and the golden sun.

Perhaps some day he would go to Vilikus and fall to his knees and beg to see those things. *Please, master, use your stone. Show me the sun. Show me the moon and the stars. And my friends, Lucie and Elsebeth. Show me their faces, because I've forg—*

Then toward the south he heard a distant shout—a *human* voice—but he couldn't understand the word. The sound made the tiny hairs on his forearms stand up straight. He ran to the southern wall and searched the gloom. Beyond the dam he saw the black silhouette of a tree fall. Water surged through the hole it crunched in the wall of sticks and mud.

At the dam murglins swarmed over the damaged area like frenzied ants. *The lake must be losing water fast*, Rudi thought. He leaned out over the wall and looked down at the edge of the tower island. He thought he might see the water receding from the shore. Instead he saw something he could not quite believe.

Far below, Hansel crouched between two boulders at the water's edge, looking up and waving. Rudi froze, wondering why on earth he'd come back. He shook his head at Hansel. *What's the matter with you?*

Hansel shook his own head in reply. He pointed at the tower, out at the forest, held his hands out like scratching claws, and drew a finger across his throat. *What does that mean? Death in the tower? Murder in the forest?* Rudi shrugged and raised his hands, palms up.

Hansel slapped his forehead. He pointed again—this time toward a place near the bottom of the tower. Rudi leaned out and saw, close to the ground, a tiny slitlike window that he hadn't realized was there—a kind of peephole in the first story. He nodded at Hansel, just in time to see him crouch low behind the boulders.

A cluster of twinkling red lights appeared below, and Vilikus stepped out of the tower's lone door. The warlock peered at the dam, and finally walked across the bridge to the prison island, where he could get a better look at the commotion. *If you're going to go, do it now, Hansel,* Rudi thought. He watched Hansel creep out from behind the boulders and slink toward the tower.

Rudi turned around to see the little murglin staring suspiciously with its neck craned forward and its eyelids half closed over the bulging eyes. Rudi walked past it, frowning. *How am I supposed to talk to Hansel with you following me around?*

One solution occurred to him. On his way down he stopped at the third floor and walked into the library.

The little murglin came after him. It looked both curious and cross.

Rudi pointed over its shoulder. "Your master wants you," he said. The murglin turned to look, and Rudi seized it by the neck at one end and the tail at the other. The creature writhed like a snake and snapped its jaws at the air. Rudi threw it into the nearest crate and slammed it closed. The murglin squealed—not in surprise, but in pain. Rudi realized that its knobby fingers were caught under the lid.

"Sorry," Rudi said. He lifted the lid a hair's width, and the fingers disappeared into the crate. He leaned on the lid and secured the latch. The crate shook and the murglin howled inside, but nobody would hear its muffled cry unless they entered the room. Rudi ran down the stairs to the first floor, where Hansel would be waiting at the narrow window.

The tower door was open. Through it, Rudi could see the warlock and his red constellation on the prison island. A single murglin stood outside to guard the entrance. But its attention too was on the dam.

Rudi looked around for the window and didn't see it. He realized it must be behind the wooden barrels. Moving quietly, he walked behind the stack. There was just enough room to squeeze through. When he reached the window—a vertical slot just six inches wide— Hansel's face popped up on the other side. Rudi was so startled he almost cried out. Part of him was happy to see

Hansel. But most of him was alarmed. By coming back, Hansel jeopardized everything—even the lives of Lucie and Elsie.

"What are you doing here? We had an agreement!" Rudi whispered.

"That agreement is broken, Rudi. Vilikus never meant to keep it. He sent his creatures to kill us as soon as we were out of sight."

Rudi felt dizzy. "What? But where are the girls? And the other children?"

Hansel checked to his left and right, like a bird watching for cats. "They're safe, on their way back to the village. Burck and the fathers have them."

"The fathers came back? Good! What about Marusch? And Uncle Hempel? Oh, Hansel, I was wrong about everything. I treated him so badly . . ."

"I don't know where they are now, Rudi. But we've arranged a place to meet, if we get out of here alive. Now come on!"

Rudi shook his head. "The door is guarded. There's no other way out."

"Just one murglin?"

Rudi peered out from behind the barrels. "Yes."

Hansel showed Rudi a short club that Tobias had given him. It shook as he held it. "Get its attention. I'll sneak up behind."

Rudi almost laughed. "You, Hansel? Hit someone with a cudgel?"

Hansel smiled back. "Can you believe it? Go on—let's get you out of here while Vilikus is busy."

Rudi walked out from behind the barrels. The floor was oily around the basin where Vilikus had soaked, and his foot slipped out to one side. The skidding sound caught the murglin guard's attention. It turned toward him and raised its spear.

With his leg out in an awkward position, Rudi decided to make the best of it. He seized his thigh and moaned. "Ow! I've hurt my leg!"

The murglin examined Rudi with a single black eye. It stepped over the threshold. Hansel appeared behind it, with his cudgel raised to strike, but it whirled about, and might have speared Hansel if the tip of its weapon hadn't caught on the side of the door. Hansel struck at it, but the murglin craned its long neck to one side, and the cudgel only grazed it.

Hansel grabbed the spear with one hand to keep from being stabbed. As he raised the other to strike with the cudgel, the murglin's head snapped forward like a snake. Its jaws clamped Hansel's elbow. He screamed through gritted teeth and dropped the cudgel.

Rudi grabbed it off the floor and struck the murglin hard on the back of its head. It took two wobbly steps outside and sagged to the ground. Hansel grimaced and held his arm.

"Come on!" Rudi said. They ran out the tower door and stopped abruptly, sending little pebbles flying with their heels.

Twenty murglins with twenty sharp spears surrounded them in a lethal crescent. And beyond the creatures, Rudi saw doom approaching: The warlock rushed toward them from the prison isle, with his skeletal legs stabbing at the ground. His fireflies lagged behind him like the sweeping tail of a fiery comet.

"Rudiger, poor Rudiger!" Vilikus called out. His voice was filled with frosty disdain.

The murglins took a step closer.

"Back inside," Rudi said. He turned and his mouth dropped open. The door was gone.

"What—where's the opening?" Hansel said.

Rudi gaped at the solid, curving wall of stone. Then the answer came.

"It's still there, Hansel—he's not letting us see it!" He held his arms out where he thought the opening should be and watched, amazed, as his hands passed through the stone slab before him.

"Come on!" he cried. He pulled Hansel by the sleeve. They stepped through the illusion and back into the tower.

The moment they were inside, the false stone vanished. Through the open doorway Rudi saw Vilikus storm across the bridge to the tower island, with the Illusion Stone cupped in his hands. The warlock's head was tilted forward, and he bared his teeth like a wolf. Just outside the threshold, the surrounding murglins had moved close together in such eerie precision that their shoulders touched.

Rudi reached for the door to close it but pulled his hand back with a shocked cry. The door was covered with razor-sharp quills that looked as if they would tear his skin to shreds at the slightest touch. He closed his eyes. *It isn't real,* he told himself, and reached without looking. He grabbed the heavy door with both hands—there was no pain, just the rough feel of the wood—and slammed it closed. Then he felt for the heavy bolt, still without opening his eyes, and slid it into place.

"We're in a lot of trouble," he said to Hansel.

"'Trapped ourselves, didn't we?" Hansel said. He used his sleeve to mop moisture off his forehead—rain, sweat, or both.

"Are you sorry you came back? You could have gotten away."

"I don't regret it, Rudi, not any of it."

"It's going to get bad now." Rudi crossed his arms and shivered.

"Just don't believe your eyes. Come to think of it, I don't suppose those murglins just now were real either," Hansel said.

Rudi's brow creased. *Of course they weren't,* he thought. *Fooled again.* Hansel made a quiet choking sound and pointed at the door. Rudi turned in time to see Vilikus appear. The warlock simply walked through the solid wood of the door.

"Poor Rudiger. I had such hopes for you," he heard

Vilikus say. The warlock loomed right before them, but the voice came from somewhere else. *The other side of the door.*

"That's not really him!" Rudi whispered to Hansel. "I know I locked that door! The real Vilikus is still outside."

The phantom warlock turned to Hansel, who stared back, white faced. "And here is clever Hansel, the one I should thank for bringing me my stone." The phantom's lips mimed the words that came from outside the tower. "What should I conjure for you next, my friend? No, don't tell me—I've heard your story. I know what you like to see."

Hansel gaped as the inside of the tower was transformed. The slabs of stone turned a rich brown. The texture softened and the hard edges rounded off. *Gingerbread*, Rudi thought.

The illusion blossomed. White frosting oozed up in the seams between the slabs. The stone basin that was full of oil now overflowed with sugar plums and candied lemon peel and honey sweets.

"Such a lovely trap for little girls and boys. But it's not for you anymore, my friend," Vilikus said. And suddenly the gingerbread and candies were covered with flies and wriggling worms. The air was filled with the sound of buzzing and munching.

Rudi jumped as the heavy door shook in its frame. Someone was trying to open it from the outside. "So you managed to bolt the door. I suppose I will need help knocking it down," the warlock said wearily.

There was a long silence.

"Is there another way out?" Hansel asked quietly, as if the phantom Vilikus might overhear him. Rudi shook his head.

The illusion stared down at them and grinned. Hansel raised his hand to block it from view. He looked around the room and noticed the strange basin and the barrels. "What's all this for?"

"He soaks himself in that oily stuff, whatever it is. It's part of his secret—how he's lived all these years."

"And those barrels—they're all filled with this oil?" Hansel said, his voice rising.

Rudi saw Hansel's face light up with understanding. But before Hansel could say another word, an ominous sound came from outside the tower. To Rudi it sounded like sloshing, splashing, and sheets of water pouring into the lake. Something enormous must have heaved itself onto land. Great plodding steps shook the floor, and a low, burbling growl made Rudi's ribs quiver.

"When the she-murg feeds this time," Vilikus thundered from outside the tower, "it will be no illusion!" The phantom's mouthed opened wide to mime the words again.

There was a deafening crash, and the door bulged like someone's chest filling with air. The she-murg roared.

"We'd better go up, away from that beast!" Hansel said. He ran for the stairs.

"Wait," Rudi cried, running after him. "What were you going to say about the oil?"

Hansel had nearly reached the second-floor landing. "I almost forgot," he called out. "Don't you see, Rudi? Why he makes it rain? Why he—" Suddenly a figure stepped out of the shadows swinging a long, curved sword.

CHAPTER 23

Hansel saw the blade and stumbled back as it whistled through the air. His heel dipped over the edge of the stairs and the rest of him followed. He landed on his back on the table below, and then he rolled onto the floor, moaning.

Agnes laughed.

Rudi screamed at her, too furious to form words. He clenched his fists so hard that it pained him.

"There goes your temper again," Agnes said, mocking him. She moved down the steps with the sword pointed at Rudi.

She's right, Rudi realized as he backed down the stairs. He couldn't lose his wits to a red rage now. Hansel had been about to reveal something important. *What was he trying to tell me? Think!*

There was another thunderous crash, and a wrenching, splintering sound. It buckled the three iron bands that ran across the door and opened a jagged crack down the middle.

"Don't you see, Rudi? Why he makes it rain?" Rudi had wondered about that himself. Was it really for the murglins, and to fill the lake? And there were other nagging mysteries, connected, perhaps, by a common thread that he'd missed until now.

Why do the ceilings let the rain in? Why are the ovens so far from the tower? Why does Vilikus need fireflies to light his way? Why no candles or torches?

A third crash came, and the door flew across the room in pieces.

At the open threshold the she-murg roared. Her cavernous mouth bristled with yellow spikes and ended in a glistening, quivering white throat. She tried to come in, but her head was too broad to squeeze through. With a hiss, she backed away, and the true warlock stepped into the tower. His limbs creaked with every motion.

Vilikus walked through his twin phantom, and it melted into him and vanished. The warlock's red eyes darted from Hansel on the floor, half conscious, to Rudi on the stairs, edging away from the sword that Agnes held.

"So tragic," Vilikus said. "The plans were crafted so carefully. You never would have known they were gone, Rudiger."

"You're a liar!" Rudi cried. "My promise was real, and yours was a lie—like your illusions." He turned to Agnes. "And are you even here? Or are you just another lie?"

"I'm here, little man," Agnes said. The point of the

sword circled before Rudi's face. "You only thought I was headed back to the village, to take the girls in. But they weren't supposed to be around that long."

Hansel groaned. He pressed his hands against the floor and pushed himself to his knees. "The oil, Rudi . . . ," he said, grimacing. Vilikus swept across the room and seized him before he could say another word. The warlock clapped his palm over Hansel's mouth, and wrapped his spindly fingers around his head. Vilikus lifted him by the skull until Hansel's outstretched toes just brushed the ground.

"Enough of you, Hansel," the warlock said icily. "You and your friends denied me a feast when you saved those children. Where are the others now—lurking about to make trouble?"

"Don't hurt him!" Rudi cried. He ran the rest of the way down the steps and fell to his knees in front of Vilikus. He lowered his head to the ground, as if worshiping the warlock.

Vilikus sneered down at him. "It's too late for pleas, Rudiger. You could have led a privileged life, endless days of learning and power. But now Hansel will feed the she-murg, who waits outside for her reward. And you, Rudi? You will feed *me*."

While Rudi was bent low, he'd reached into his pocket for the flint and steel. *Is this it, Hansel? Is this the answer?* He prayed it was. Now his right hand was in the band of steel, and he struck it hard across the stone. Hot sparks flew like shooting stars onto the warlock's robe. Flames blossomed where every spark landed.

Vilikus shrieked. He let go of Hansel and batted at the fire with both hands. Rudi edged as close as he dared and struck the flint again and again. Specks of flaming steel shot onto the warlock's sleeves, legs, and chest. Vilikus tried in vain to snuff them.

"That's why you make it rain! To keep you safe from fire!" Rudi screamed.

Hansel wobbled to his feet and grabbed Rudi by the arm. "Smart boy," he said hoarsely. "Time to run!"

When they turned, Agnes and her sword were there. "What have you done?" she cried. The blade shook as she gawked at her master.

Vilikus staggered. He stepped in a pool of oil and a blue flame spread around his feet. It rippled across the floor, and the flames crawled up the side of the stone basin, toward the deep pool of oil.

Agnes saw disaster looming and ran out the doorway. Then she spun and tried to come back with a wild, frightened look in her eyes. The she-murg was waiting for her meal. Agnes fell into the shadow of her cavernous mouth. The creature's jaws snapped shut, and the last Rudi saw of his wicked aunt was the shoe flying loose from her foot.

Vilikus howled. The fireflies still swirled around him, obedient to the end. One by one they burst into flame and fell.

"We have to get out!" Hansel shouted. Vilikus turned at the sound and came for them, grasping blindly. Then he simply crumbled before them, with the hot air shimmering around him and a liquid cloud of black smoke billowing up.

Hansel pushed Rudi toward the door, but the way out was blocked by the she-murg, who eyed them hungrily. They ran for the stairs instead. Behind them the fire reached the basin, and an eruption of heat and light gushed up from the pool of oil and stabbed through the latticed ceiling above. On the floor the flames licked at the stack of barrels.

They mounted the stairs, pressing themselves against the wall to avoid the heat. The flames rose with them.

"Looks like we're in the oven again, Rudi!" Hansel shouted.

Rudi had felt a moment of elation over the fiery fate of the warlock, but it was swept aside by the raw panic he felt now. They could run, but there was no escape from this inferno.

At the third floor Rudi pulled at Hansel's arm to stop him.

"Wait, Hansel!" he shouted. He ran to one of the crates, flipped the latch, and lifted the lid. The tiny murglin hopped out and poised on the edge of the box. Rudi sensed a difference in the creature—it seemed more like a frightened animal than the sinister servant it had been. When it felt the heat of the flames, the murglin leaped off the crate and bounded through a window. Rudi wished they could exit the same way but the space was too narrow.

They climbed on and reached the top of the tower. From below there came a series of earsplitting pops—the barrels exploding, and the oil inside igniting. A ball of flame billowed high into the night sky.

Rudi turned his face from the searing heat and covered his head with one elbow. "We have to jump!" he shouted.

"We'll break our necks!" Hansel shouted back.

No doubt, Rudi thought. The stone-studded ground was far below, distant enough to break every bone in his body if he leaped. But soon they'd have no choice. The heat was too strong.

Something flashed in the corner of his eye, and he heard a high-pitched clatter amid the roaring wind: wood on stone.

It was an arrow, with a rope knotted around its shaft—a mooring line from one of the murglin boats. Hansel laughed and slapped Rudi on the back. "She never gives up!" He slipped the rope into a notch at the edge of the wall, where the arrow would lie sideways and keep it secure. "You first, little cousin!"

Rudi slid down the rope, past windows that spit flame like the mouths of dragons. *What friends I have,* he thought. *What friends . . .*

* * *

The boat skimmed across the lake, away from the raging vessel of fire that the tower had become. "Look," Marusch said as they passed an islet where a pair of murglins stood. One of them looked curiously at the spear in its hands, as if it didn't recognize the object, or what it was for. The other stared dully at them as they passed. The gleam of intelligence had left its eyes.

There was a sound like thunder behind them, and Rudi turned around to watch the tower slowly collapse. The walls sagged and fell inward, the immense slabs rumbled together, and the warlock's tower became a heap of smoking rock.

"Good," Hansel said, nodding. "The last thing I wanted to do was go back and sift through the ashes for that accursed stone. It would take a hundred men to dig it out now, even if they knew where to look. Let it rest there forever."

Around them bits of ash and flaming parchment floated down and hissed on the still surface of the lake. "All his books and scrolls," Rudi said.

"The world won't miss that knowledge," Hansel replied.

Marusch turned her face toward the sky. "The rain has stopped."

Rudi put his hands out. No fine mist settled on his skin. He looked up and saw gaps in the cloud where stars twinkled.

The boat scraped against the shore, and the three of them hopped out. Marusch led them to the foot of the stony peak where they'd fought off the murglins.

She framed her mouth with her hands and called out three times for Hempel, in a voice that was clear and strong.

No answer. The woods were perfectly still.

CHAPTER 24

"He's not coming, is he?" Rudi asked. All the joy he'd felt at their escape had suddenly evaporated.

Hansel blinked slowly and lowered his head. "He felled a tree into the dam, Rudi. To distract the murglins, so we could get to you."

"I . . . I think I heard him," said Rudi.

"We agreed to meet here when it was over," Marusch said quietly.

A sound came from the trees. They turned their heads in unison as a sturdy figure caked in mud hobbled into the clearing. Even its face was covered with brown muck. A pair of bright eyes blinked at them. "I'm coming," Hempel said wearily. "I nearly drowned when the dam broke. You should have seen those murglins run. . . ."

Rudi made an odd noise, somewhere between a laugh and a whimper. He raced to Hempel and wrapped his arms around his waist, trying but failing to lift his uncle off the ground.

Hempel tousled Rudi's blond hair, smearing it with dirt. "There, there, Rudi. What's the matter, Nephew? You're not crying, are you? But we made it, Rudi. Every one of us made it." Rudi pressed his face into his uncle's muddy chest and squeezed him tighter still. Hempel looked at Marusch and Hansel, confused for a moment, and then he smiled, wide and bright.

CHAPTER 25

They stood under the great tree where Marusch had dwelled, and looked at the wreckage of her home on the forest floor.

"I can rebuild it," Marusch said.

"Let me help you," Hempel said.

Marusch looked at him with one eyebrow raised high. "You don't have to do that. You must be eager to return to your home."

"Well ... not especially. Hansel is taking Rudi and the girls to Kurahaven. But a city like that is not for me. I was rather hoping ..." Hempel's lip trembled.

Now both of Marusch's eyebrows arched high. "Hoping what? Tell me, Hempel."

Hempel's reply was almost too quiet to hear. "Hoping that I could stay with you. Even after we fix things, I mean. If ... if you don't mind."

Marusch stared at him, astounded, and didn't answer

for the longest time. Hempel's head sagged forward until his nose pointed at the ground.

"I don't mind," Marusch said at last, barely loud enough to hear. "If you really wish to stay."

Hempel's head sprang up again, and he clapped his hands together. "Well, then—let's get started!" He began to collect the fallen pieces of Marusch's dwelling, humming happily to himself. Marusch took a few wobbly steps toward the nearest tree and leaned against it.

"It's the queerest thing," Hansel said softly. He turned to meet Rudi's questioning glance. "Do you know I actually feel a little jealous?"

Something occurred to Marusch. "Wait here," she called to Rudi, and ran into the forest. She was back in a minute with a small leather pouch, and she tossed it to Rudi.

"Take this back," she said. "You left it in my tree."

Rudi pried the top open and looked inside. His jaw dropped. He'd forgotten completely.

"I told you, I have no use for such things," she said, smiling.

The next day, in a village many miles down the road from Waldrand, Rudi, Hansel, and the girls waited for the cart that Hansel had hired. Overhead a few shreds of cloud drifted aimlessly away from the forest, perhaps the last remnants of the storm that Vilikus had conjured.

This time nothing dreadful happened before they

could leave, and the four of them settled in for the long journey that would take them around the forest and north to Kurahaven, the city by the sea.

They traveled for days along the edge of the woods. The road curved always to the left, orbiting the forest in a great arc. The wagons they hired clattered along, first heading east, then easing northeast, then north, then northwest. It seemed to Rudi that they were held on a long string, with the other end still tethered to that smoldering rubble in the warlock's lake.

They stayed in villages along the road at night, and each one seemed a little bigger, a little busier than the last. Rudi couldn't sleep well in the inns, especially when his room faced the wall of trees. He'd sit at the window with his chin on his folded arms and stare at the moon-lit trees, waiting for dark forms to creep out. It was eas-ier to doze in the wagon the next morning, lulled by the rhythmic clomp of hooves.

Finally—finally!—the road turned north again, peel-ing away from the forest. The string snapped and they were free. Rudi gazed back and watched the forest recede like a passing storm. He looked at Hansel and the girls. They were smiling.

"Is that it, Hansel? Is that Kurahaven?" Elsebeth said, pointing ahead. Rudi's eyes widened as he saw in the distance a dense cluster of colorful buildings.

Hansel glanced and chuckled. "That little burg? Heavens, no. It's a lovely stop along the way. But it's a speck on the map compared to where we're going."

They stayed the night in a cheery inn in that little burg. Long before dawn Rudi's eyes fluttered open. He sat up in his bed, feeling restless and strange. He wondered if he'd eaten too much at dinner—a full stomach was still a novelty for him. Finally, knowing he wouldn't fall asleep again, he got up quietly, crept past the beds where the girls slept, and slipped out the door.

There was a common room downstairs. He was glad nobody else sat there; he didn't feel like talking. Rudi walked to the hearth, where a few orange embers still glowed from the fire the innkeeper had made the night before.

He saw a bucket of water next to the hearth. An impulse came to him, and he tipped the bucket over the embers, pouring the water slowly at first, careful to hit every spot where the coals still burned. They hissed and popped and smoked as the water doused the last traces of the fire. He emptied the entire bucket, just to be sure.

Rudi pursed his lips and nodded as he kneeled before the hearth, watching the gray ashes cool. Finally he yawned and stretched, returned to his room, and fell into a deep and easy sleep.

Two days later the road was busier than ever with carts and wagons. One passed them with a load of staring silver fish. There was a foreign scent in the air, brought to Rudi's nose by a warm breeze from ahead. Large white birds with gray wings and pale orange feet soared effortlessly above. *Gulls*, Hansel called them. Their haunting cry was so different from the chirp and tweet of forest birds.

Just before the cart crested a steep rise in the road, Hansel said, "Rudi, Elsebeth, Lucie: Close your eyes." And a moment later, "Now open them."

Before them stood Kurahaven, a mile away at the end of the gently descending road. It was even grander than Rudi had imagined: a riot of spires and columns and arches and bridges and walls and domes. Beyond it the blue sea dazzled under the sun, freckled with the geometric sails of a hundred ships and studded with countless islands as far as the horizon. Rudi blinked, hardly able to take it all in.

Beyond the great towers and before the bustling port where the ships docked, cheerfully painted houses lined the winding streets, three stories high and touching each other to form a long solid wall. At one of these Hansel asked the driver to stop the cart at last.

"Here it is," Hansel said. "My home." Rudi wondered why he was frowning.

Hansel stared at the windows, which were open to the breeze. The windowsills were filled with boxes of flowers. "Someone's here," he said.

A head popped out a window of the house next door. It was a bald, jowly man with white whiskers. "Say, neighbor, you're back! With company, I see. Well, she got here a few days after you left. I didn't think you'd mind if I let her in."

Hansel's brow wrinkled. "What? Who, Gruber? Who did you let in?"

Before Gruber could answer, the front door to Hansel's house opened. Hansel stared dumbstruck, as a woman stepped onto the top step and wavered there. She was dressed in a lovely gown, red laced with gold. Her hair was half brown and half gray, like Hansel's. She put her fingers to her lips, and a tear raced past her smiling mouth.

"Is that your wife, Hansel?" asked Elsebeth.

"I . . . I don't have a wife," Hansel said. "But I have a sister." And he rushed up the stairs as Gretel ran down, and they met in the middle and embraced.

"Isn't that a thing," said Lucie.

Rudi and the girls sat on the steps. Hansel had sent the driver off and asked them to wait outside for a moment. That seemed like an hour ago. Hansel's neighbor Gruber, a gossipy fellow, leaned out his window and told them what he knew about Gretel. Her husband was the captain of a ship that must have been lost at sea. Gretel waited many years for him to return, until she finally decided to come back to Kurahaven and find her brother again.

The door to Hansel's house opened and Gretel emerged. Rudi thought she looked as if she had a kind face and a good heart. She sat beside them with her long dress flowing across the steps.

"You've all had quite an adventure, haven't you?" Gretel said. "Hansel tells me we must find a home for you three. And that is a simple matter: You will stay here with us. Hansel wasn't sure he could manage you by himself, but now that I'm here, he needn't worry about that. But of course, it's up to you if you want to stay. Do you think you'd be happy here?"

Hansel reappeared at the top of the stairs. He smiled and nodded at Rudi and the girls, and dabbed the corner of one eye with his little finger.

Rudi felt a warm glow in his veins. But it wasn't like the hateful, all-consuming fire that had haunted him for so long. It wasn't like that at all.

He had to clear his throat before he could reply.

"Well," he said, smiling, "I think we'll live as happily as can be expected."

Coming soon, the next adventure from P. W. Catanese.

The Mirror's Tale

Twin brothers Albert and William, descendants of the princess known as Snow White, are both heirs to the Ambercrest throne. But only one will rule. . . .

Available Summer 2006

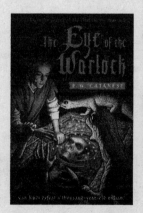

PENDRAGON

Bobby Pendragon is a seemingly normal fourteen-year-old boy. He has a family, a home, and a possible new girlfriend. But something happens to Bobby that changes his life forever.

HE IS CHOSEN TO DETERMINE THE COURSE OF HUMAN EXISTENCE.

Pulled away from the comfort of his family and suburban home, Bobby is launched into the middle of an immense, interdimensional conflict involving racial tensions, threatened ecosystems, and more. It's a journey of danger and discovery for Bobby, and his success or failure will do nothing less than determine the fate of the world. . . .

PENDRAGON

by D. J. MacHale

Book One: The Merchant of Death
Book Two: The Lost City of Faar
Book Three: The Never War
Book Four: The Reality Bug
Book Five: Black Water

Coming Soon: Book Six: The Rivers of Zadaa

From Aladdin Paperbacks • Published by Simon & Schuster